Apparitions
Anonymous

Rachel Poli

For Grandpa, Theresa, Paul, Pa, Denise, Granddad, & Sandra

Foreword

Written by The Grim Reaper

A round wooden table seating two fills an otherwise empty room. The table sits beside a frameless window, appearing as a hole in the wall, but I'll let you in on a little secret. There are no windows. No walls. Only the void of the Afterlife.

But don't let that alarm you. The Afterlife is harmless; I assure you. This room is where I hold Crossover Sessions between myself and those arriving to the Afterlife. Those being spirits, of course.

I'm the Grim Reaper, overseer of the Afterlife, and all those who cross over.

Don't be frightened; I've heard all the rumors about me those in the Living World created. I'm not entirely sure why they've chosen to pick on me, but I can confidently say those rumors are untrue.

Yes, I wear a long, black cloak. There isn't much color here.

Yes, my hood covers my face. A soul separated from its living form isn't so pretty to look at.

Yes, I carry a scythe. I found it somewhere and thought it looked cool.

I'm an ordinary soul trying to help other spirits understand where they are, why they're here, and what to do next, because there's more to life after death.

That's another common rumor that's simply not true. Death does not mean you stop living. It's a new chapter. A new journey. You may not be able to do everything you once did in the Living World, but new experiences are waiting for you.

I sit in this room among newly departed souls, helping them understand their previous lives, their current death, and how to live their lives in death.

I've gathered my files from some Crossover Sessions to share with you. Why? Because you're still in the Living World, and I hope these spirits' stories help you on your own journey. Live your life to the fullest. Take nothing for granted. Enjoy every moment.

Welcome to Apparitions Anonymous. It may not look like much, but I hope to create a comfortable experience for you. So, please, choose a warm beverage, pull up a chair, and let's begin.

CONTENTS

THE FIRST GROUP

A SOUL ENTERED, HIS face scanning the empty room with wide eyes. He sat in the chair seated across from me at the round table, head bowed, fingers intertwining with one another—at least, they would if his hands were solid. Instead, his fingers passed through each other. However, there was nothing else for him to look at other than me.

And he refused to look in my direction.

"Do you drink coffee?" I asked.

He shook his head, still not looking at me.

"Tea?"

Another head shake. This time he waved his hands, watching one pass through the other.

"Hot chocolate?" I asked, making one appear before him.

It wasn't often a young soul crossed over, but it happened more often than you'd think. This gentleman before me perished at 27 years old, dying from a car accident. It wasn't his fault, so it seemed he was in the wrong place at the wrong time. At least, that's what most people told themselves to justify such an accident.

The soul leaned forward, taking a whiff of the hot chocolate. He cupped the mug in his hands, and I noticed his brows furrow. I smiled, knowing he became confused about his hands being able to touch the mug. Our spirits were physical when they needed to be, though I didn't explain this. I wanted him to come to me with questions.

He didn't take a sip of the drink, which was alright with me. I hoped he'd find some comfort in the drink's warmth and sweet scent all the same.

"Are you feeling better?" I asked gently.

I knew the answer. Of course he wasn't. Hot chocolate doesn't fix everything, even though it should.

He finally glanced in my direction. Progress.

We locked eyes for a moment before he tore his gaze away. I knew he saw the abyss under my dark hood and now he shook, his hands fidgeting once more. Now I understood what the issue was.

"You're in a safe space here. I know it's intimidating at first, but you're alright. I'm here to help."

His head lifted once more, slow. Hesitation filled his open mouth before he finally stammered out some words. "Help?"

There was a hint of surprise in his tone, and I couldn't help but chuckle. I nodded. "Yes."

"But aren't you the...?"

"I am."

"Then how...?"

Here we go. The rumors about me from the Living World always carried over with the newly departed spirits. Despite my helping them arrive at the Afterlife in the first place, they were still afraid of me, all because of an assumption. All living beings are judgmental. It's in their nature and very few of them grow out of it overtime.

"Everything you learned about me when you were alive isn't true. I don't know how those rumors started in the first place, but I'm the Grim Reaper, not death. I help souls like you cross over from the Living World to the Spirit World. This room," I explained, pointing to the emptiness surrounding us, "is where souls come to talk if they're feeling troubled, don't know what to do next, or maybe they want to relive happy memories from when they were alive."

The young man leaned back in his chair, still tightly gripping his mug. He nodded along, though I felt unsure if any of my words sunk in.

He drew in a sharp breath, breathing in the beverage's scent once more before frowning, his gaze watching the rich chocolate swirl around.

"I'm scared," was all he said, his voice meek like a child who had a nightmare in the middle of the night.

I cracked an encouraging smile. "It's okay to be scared. Perfectly normal. Would you like to elaborate on those feelings?"

I knew what he was afraid of. This place. Death. Me. Next steps. But I needed him to say it out loud. He had to admit it. Otherwise, I couldn't help.

This was the hard part of conducting these sessions. I wasn't allowed to put thoughts into the spirits' minds. Whatever they thought, whatever they felt, they had to admit. They needed to arrive to their own conclusions or else they could never truly rest in peace. If it's my idea, they'll only do what they think they're *supposed* to do, not what's best for them.

The soul didn't answer me. Instead, he cast a somber gaze out the window into the nothingness beyond.

"Do you have questions about this place?" I prompted.

Now he looked at me, his expression curious. He stared at my face as though he were suddenly unafraid. "I don't know where I am. How I got here, who you are, or why I had to die. I don't even remember... wait," he paused, holding up an index finger, "there was a car accident, wasn't there?"

I nodded.

He put his mug down on the table, using his hands to reenact the moment of the accident. "A car came toward me. I tried to brake, but I don't think I stopped. Nothing stopped. I don't remember feeling pain. Is that," he swallowed, "is that how I died?"

I nodded again.

"So, I'm here because I wasn't a good person when I was alive?"

Another rumor from the Living World. Some people believed if you were bad, you'd go underground. If you were good, you'd go to the sky. The truth is, everyone went into the ground unless they choose to turn to ash.

"You're here because you're dead," I stated. "There is no good or bad place, up or down, whatever you learned in the physical world. This place, the Afterlife, is where everyone goes when they become one with their spirit form again. I bring all the souls here to help them cross over peacefully so none wander aimlessly and unaware in the Living World. I helped you find the Afterlife and now I'll help you find peace and decide what to do next."

He tilted his head to the side, a brow raised. "What to do next? I'm dead. Surely there isn't anything I can do now?"

"Just because you're dead doesn't mean you stop living," I replied.

The young man sighed, slouching in his seat. "But I can't live the way I did before. I was so close to finishing my degree. My life was finally starting over and now my life *is* over. What could I possibly do here?"

I shrugged nonchalantly. "There are many things you can do here. You can go back to the physical world from time to time to check in on your loved ones."

"I don't know. I feel like it's too soon for that."

"You can stay here, roam around. See what the Afterlife offers and meet some other souls. Maybe you'll find some loved ones who have passed on long before you."

At those words, the young soul looked worried again. Maybe I had said too much, overwhelming him with things he could do.

The large clock that rested above the door frame where the soul entered turned orange, enveloping the room in a warm hue.

The spirit jumped, startled. "What's that?"

"The Clock. Orange means our time is almost up for the session," I explained. Although, I felt our conversation was far from over. The gentleman was still unsure, still afraid.

"Has that been here the whole time?" he asked.

"Yes."

"Clearly, there's a lot I have to learn about this place." He stood. "Maybe I will wander the Afterlife and check things out."

The Clock turned red.

It was abrupt, but I didn't question it. I stood, too. "Please don't hesitate to come back if you need to talk."

All he did was nod and then exit underneath The Clock, his silhouette fading into the distance. As soon as his spirit disappeared, The Clock turned yellow. Another soul waited their turn to enter the Crossover Room.

***

I allowed the next soul to enter the Crossover Room. Their spirit staggered over to the table, as though they couldn't remember how their legs worked. They'd soon find it easier to levitate, but it often took time for the apparitions to realize they could do such a thing.

This soul was an elderly woman. She took her time getting to the table and, when she sat down, The Clock turned green. The session had begun.

"Tea? Coffee?" I offered.

"Tea, please." Her voice was throaty with age.

I flicked my wrist and a cup of steaming tea appeared in front of her, and myself as well. I could no longer taste it, but having a warm beverage helped with the cozy ambiance.

The woman cupped her mug with both frail hands, taking a sip. Soon, she'd no longer be able to taste it, though she seemed satisfied as of now.

"So," she began, placing her mug back onto the table, "where did you bring me?"

"You're in the Afterlife, or Spirit World," I explained frankly.

The spirit before me left her physical form behind in a hospital bed. I watched the whole thing, knowing her time neared the end. When her soul detached, we didn't linger long before heading to the Afterlife together.

When she had died, she immediately came with me, no questions asked. That happened sometimes. The soul is in such shock that they'll do whatever you ask of them. They don't question why they can see themselves outside their body. There are no questions about where they're going or why. They don't even recognize who I am until we arrive in the Spirit World.

Every soul acts differently immediately after death. In these cases, something deep inside them knows it's time for them to go.

"It's not much, is it?" her plain tone broke me out of my thoughts.

I followed her gaze around the empty room. "No, I suppose not. Although, most spirits don't spend much time here. They go back to the Living World to watch over their loved ones."

The woman growled into her mug. "Not me," she said after taking a sip of tea. "I can't see my family now."

I frowned. "Why not?"

"I spent my last few months in a hospital room, not being able to advocate for myself. I could barely speak, let alone keep my eyes open. My daughters visited me, talked to me... but I couldn't return the conversation. I was a limp fish out of water. Embarrassing." She glared into the mug now as though it were the drink's fault. I spoke up before she threw it.

I had a spirit do that once. They were so confused and angry; they threw the mug like a baseball toward the wall where The Clock sat. Except there are no walls and nothing here is truly physical. So, when the mug faded into the distance with no satisfying clatter of glass, the spirit had sat back down, more puzzled than before.

"Your family still came to visit you," I recounted. "They wanted to be with you and wanted you to have the company."

She snorted. "They shouldn't have paused their lives to ensure someone came to visit me in the hospital. I was such a burden. A lost cause."

I hummed to myself, watching her take another sip. "I don't think that at all," I said. She arched a brow over her mug at me.

"If you were a burden, I don't think any family member would see you. They wouldn't have made the effort. Otherwise, what could you do about it? Nothing. You couldn't. I'm sure they were aware you knew they were present, even though you weren't able to open your eyes."

"Eh," she shrugged, brushing aside my words. She put her mug down, straightening her posture. Her demeanor changed as she looked the other way defiantly. "I'm 85. It was my time to go, not theirs."

"They didn't go anywhere," I replied, a bit confused.

She looked at me, and I noticed a glint of amusement in her eyes. "Not physically, no, but they wasted much of their time sitting around that filthy hospital room. It wasn't fair to them. They should have just let me go."

She took another quick sip of her tea before putting it on the table once more. It was then I realized she hadn't really been drinking it at all.

"You can't pause love," I said, watching the ripples spread inside her cup. "Whatever state you're in—mentally, physically, or emotionally—those who love you will always come back."

I heard the spirit sigh and cast my gaze back to her. She now looked out the window into the void. I brought my tea to my lips, unsure if my words sunk in. Assuming I said too much, I figured I'd let her come to me.

But then she spoke, her words just as dull as our surroundings.

"I wasn't a good mom, you know. I'd forget appointments. Miss dance recitals. I'd make them walk home when I didn't feel like picking them up from school... sometimes I lost track of time. Keeping a job was like catching water for me. No matter how hard I tried, I couldn't do it."

"But you *did* try," I concluded.

The woman turned to face me, shock on her face. She slouched, leaning back into her chair.

"Did you have grandchildren?"

"Yes."

"Then your children know it's not easy being a parent. Juggling schedules, taking care of everybody and forgetting to take care of yourself in the process. Jobs aren't easy to come by and when you catch one, there's no guarantee it'll make you happy. Every day is different. Some are easier than others, but there are always a few steady people in your life you can count on during each of those days, no matter what."

There was a moment of silence before she looked down into her lap, smirking. She responded quietly, "Why would they be there for me when I was never there for them?"

"You tried," I repeated. "For some, blood is thicker than water, and that's all the explanation they need. For others, they knew how important they were to you. They saw you trying. You must have done something right somewhere that stuck with them for all those years."

The older woman looked up at me, her expression neutral, lifting her shoulders once more confidently. She hummed, then she snickered. "You know, this tea isn't that great."

I chuckled. "Now that you're a spirit, you'll lose your sense of taste, smell, and touch."

"That's odd," she observed.

I didn't make the rules, though she wouldn't miss her sense of taste. Spirits didn't need to eat, nor did they get hungry.

She traced the rim of her cup with an index finger. Though she looked deep in thought about something else. That's when I noticed The Clock had turned orange.

"I don't feel like I earned my children's love, let alone any forgiveness they gave me during my final days. But I guess what you speak has some truth to it. No one can argue I didn't try when they were kids. I didn't have that village everyone talked about for raising kids. I did my best and... well, I guess my best was good enough." She smiled.

The Clock turned red.

***

The gentleman spirit sitting across the table from me hummed a tune as he sipped his coffee. I watched him take a sip, peer inside the cup, then sip again. He didn't pay me any mind. I glanced at The Clock, which was still green. We had been sitting in this room for quite some time, however long that actually was.

Time was an illusion, something man-made from those in the Living World. They created time to dictate how they run their lives while alive. Whatever position the sun and moon were in, whatever numbers on their clocks showed, that's how they ran their lives.

The Clock in the Afterlife counted how long a session would last. However, it didn't hold a certain amount of time, but was based on the feelings of the spirit in this room, whether they were close to being at ease and finding their peace. The Clock was face-less, much like everything else in the Afterlife. It didn't contain numbers or hands, but changed colors instead. The colors illuminated the Crossover Room, but only dimly. Most of the time, I didn't think the spirits noticed The Clock, despite its large diameter. That was alright though; I knew the purpose of The Clock and what the colors meant. Each session was green for most of the time, before turning orange to let us know the session was close to ending. Red would end the session and yellow meant a soul waited to be let in. I didn't know why it was a clock to begin with, but I assumed it was because it was familiar to the recently departed souls.

When the man had entered the room, we politely greeted each other before I offered him a beverage. He graciously took coffee, but I couldn't tell if he enjoyed it or not. He must have been losing his sense of taste, but he still drank it contently. It was hard to tell without him speaking to me, though I didn't think he ignored me on purpose. Sometimes the spirit needed some time to process things themselves first.

"What brand is this?" he finally asked, curiosity overpowering his tone.

"Oh," I hesitated, surprised. No one had ever asked me that before. "Uh, mine."

He nodded, taking another sip before placing his mug down on the table. He leaned back in his chair, crossing one leg over the other. For a new spirit, he was oddly relaxed. "It tastes like," he smacked his lips, "it tastes like the coffee my first wife used to make."

"Really?" I replied, unsure if that was a good thing or not.

He laughed. "She was so terrible at it. Either the coffee was watered down, or you'd be chewing coffee grounds."

Now he roared with laughter, and I snickered as well. I knew why the coffee tasted off, but for now, I'd let him believe I was terrible at making coffee.

"I think my ex-wife did it on purpose sometimes. She'd always drink the coffee just fine. I mean, she seemed to enjoy it more whenever I made it, but she'd drink hers no problem. Often, I wondered if she made it better for herself and tried to ruin my morning, or if she really was that bad at making coffee and drank it out of stubbornness."

I nodded along, letting him talk. I never know much about a spirit's previous life. All I knew was how they died and when so I could guide them to the Spirit World. Whatever they did in their physical form had nothing to do with the Afterlife, despite what many of them believed.

So, it was hard to tell if these were fond memories or not, but it sure seemed like it.

But then the gentleman sighed. "I guess none of that matters now, huh? I'm here and there's no going back."

"No, but you could revisit the Living World if you wanted," I explained.

He cast me a sad smile. "I was supposed to get married again, though. I didn't think I'd be able to love again, not after my first wife. She wasn't a bad person. We just fell out of love somehow on our journey. I've seen others go through that, but never thought it would happen to me."

"It always happens to other people, yes," I said in agreement, "but that doesn't make us invincible."

He chuckled. "I guess everything happens for a reason, right?"

I nodded, even though that wasn't completely true. Everyone had a specific amount of time to live in their physical form from the moment they're born into that world. It was unclear, even to me, when someone's life was longer than another's, or why one died from old age and another passed on from an illness. As far as I was concerned, there wasn't much reason behind it at all.

He took another sip, his expression turning sour. Then he placed the cup down on the table.

"I should mention you're losing your sense of taste now that you're a spirit," I explained.

He forced a grin toward me and I didn't know why he felt the need to be so optimistic. Not that I'm complaining, of course, but I couldn't help but wonder if something else was going on in the back of his mind.

"It's alright," he said reassuringly. "Just a bit cold."

I flicked my wrist, adding more coffee to his mug to warm it up. He grabbed the mug, sipped again, and sighed happily.

The Clock turned orange. It was at that moment I realized it wasn't about the taste at all for him. His soul grew cold, and he clung onto that warm feeling. He wasn't ready to fully let go, but he understood enough.

"I find it odd that this coffee is comforting me as it reminds me of my ex-wife," he began explaining. "I'm grateful to her in so many ways. We were high school sweethearts. Maybe we got married too young. Still, I wouldn't be who I am today without her. My divorce with her put me on the path to meet my fiancé. I'm sorry I'll never get to build a life with her, but she made me feel again." He gripped his warm mug tighter, beaming at the steam rising. "Happiness, love, warmth... much like this cup of coffee."

I grinned at his words. These sessions were always the easiest. He was already at peace, even though his life may have felt incomplete. Sometimes, all the spirit needed was someone to lend an ear over a warm beverage.

The Clock turned red, and as if he knew what it meant, the spirit stood. He gulped down the rest of his coffee, exhaling with delight.

"The taste is bitter at times and may leave a sour note behind," he said, staring into the empty mug. "But if you find someone to warm it up for you, it's easier to keep going."

***

I had never done group sessions before. Meeting with a spirit one-on-one was always easiest so I could give them my undivided attention. Sometimes the souls would be at peace being here, others wouldn't. Some spirits recounted their physical life and others inquired about the things they can do and places they can go in the Spirit World. However, most of them only wanted to see loved ones again, whether they had already passed on or were still in the Living World.

A wide range of emotions always filled the space: anger, sadness, confusion, relief, joy—sometimes, all those emotions at once.

Usually, after a session, the spirit was free to do whatever they pleased. Whether they remain in the Afterlife for a while or head back to the Living World right away was up to them. Others came back for another session, still unsure of what to do. What their purpose was.

It's for this reason I decided trying group Crossover Sessions. I didn't know how well it'd go, if at all. The session would be awkward, I was sure. If spirits clashed in personality, that'd bring on a new set of issues. But I'd have to wait and see how things turned out.

Overall, the purpose of these group sessions was to understand one another and help each other out. We're a community no one knows exists.

The Clock turned yellow, signaling to me the spirits waited beyond. My time alone ended, so I let them in.

First, an older woman entered. Two men, one middle-aged and one a young adult, followed behind her. These spirits were quite the variety together, but I knew they'd be able to share their own part of wisdom and perspective.

"Welcome," I said, watching the three souls sit at the round table. Two more chairs appeared so all four of us could sit comfortably together. "Thank you for agreeing to come back for this group session. It's something new I'm testing out when helping spirits crossover."

"You mean we're not there, yet?" the young man asked, sitting down in between the other man and woman. His face filled with concern.

"No, you are," I replied, "but sometimes it's not always easy for spirits to get accustomed to this form. These sessions are to help you talk through whatever you need to get off your chest. You can recount memories from your physical form, or talk about how you arrived here. Maybe there are still some things you don't quite understand."

The three spirits nodded their heads in unison, all looking at me. I shifted in my chair, suddenly nervous. I was here to help, and they all counted on me to guide them. "Drink?" I asked.

They each agreed, and I gave them their respective drinks from their first sessions. Tea for the lady, coffee for the gentleman, and hot chocolate for the young man. For myself, a cup of coffee.

"Who would like to start the conversation?" I asked.

There was silence at first, and I wondered if this would work at all. During regular sessions, they could say whatever was on their mind to me. But now, if they had anything to say, it wasn't just to me. It was in front of an audience.

Before I could speak again, the young boy raised his hand, sheepishly slouching in his chair.

"Can I say I'm scared to be here?" he asked meekly.

"Why?" the old woman snapped, though I didn't think she meant to sound as harsh as she did. "What are you scared about?" she asked more calm.

"This place?" The boy replied, uncertainty clouding his tone. He shied away from the woman as she spoke to him.

"Do you realize where you are?" she pressed.

"The Afterlife?"

"Exactly. There's nothing to be afraid of here. You're at peace." She picked up her tea, sipping it delicately as though she didn't just shame him for his feelings. I wondered if I should intervene, but the conversation continued.

The young man said, *"At* peace? That's not a place."

"It doesn't have to be," she responded, her tone much more mild now. "It can be whatever or wherever you want it to be. The point is, you're at peace."

The young man turned to look in my direction. I think he wanted me to speak up, but I waited to see if he or the other gentleman had a response.

The thing was, the older lady wasn't wrong. She was correct that they were all at peace. However, what she failed to mention—or she probably didn't realize—was that not everyone found their peace right away. Some spirits spent a long time finding their peace after arriving here because everyone's peace was different.

For this woman, it seemed death was her peace. Yet, I had a feeling she only *thought* she knew her peace.

"What's that supposed to mean?" the middle-aged man chimed into the conversation. "Can't you see how young this boy is? Surely he can't find his peace here. Not yet."

"What peace?" the young man questioned again.

"It's nothing tangible," the gentleman replied. "It's something you feel."

"Do you feel it?"

"Not quite."

The woman sighed into her teacup. She put it down on the table, leaning closer to the young man. "I guess that was insensitive of me. How did you die?"

The young man drew in a sharp breath, sitting taller in his seat. "Well, I..." he glanced at me again and I nodded reassuringly.

"A car accident," he explained. "I don't remember much of it, but I crashed into someone head-on. I'm not even sure if anyone else died or if it was my fault."

He was the only one who died, though he didn't cause the accident. It wasn't his fault. The other car had run a red light. And, no, they didn't collide head-on. The oncoming car slammed directly into the young man's driver's side, killing him instantly. The whiplash snapped his neck.

It always fascinated me listening to a spirit recount their final moments before death, or the act of them dying, for it was always skewed. The memory did that. If it was too traumatic or they were in denial about it, then the mind remembered it differently. It was the brain's way of protecting them.

Sometimes the story of their death differed vastly from how it actually occurred. In other cases, the story was only slightly off. Then, of course, you have the ones who recount their death spot-on. I once had a woman so excited about how she died from a car accident because she enjoyed physics. The reaction of the cars upon impact fascinated her.

My point is, everyone is different. I never interfered with their retelling. It wasn't my place to correct them, but to help them come to terms with what happened to them, and to help them find their peace and rest.

"I'm sorry to hear about the accident," the gentleman stated.

"Don't apologize to him," the woman remarked. "No one did anything wrong. He's here because he's supposed to be."

The man glared at her. "Someone did something wrong if there was a car accident. Besides, he's just a kid. He most certainly should not be here. Not now, not at his age."

The woman shrugged her shoulders, picking up her tea again and holding it with both hands. "His cards were dealt. Nothing we can do about it now."

I watched as the two adults bicker and the man in his twenties slouch down in his chair like a small child. Clearly, he was uncomfortable, and I didn't blame him. I couldn't tell if this group sessions went well or not. So far, no one cried or shouted, but they seemed close to arguing. To me, it was a solid debate.

The man was correct—a young adult should not be a spirit. But then that begs the question, what is the appropriate age to join the Spirit World? If everyone knew when they'd leave their physical form, one of two things would happen.

One, some would do everything they could with their time. However, they wouldn't waste it with things that didn't appeal to them, drastically narrowing their world.

Two, some wouldn't do anything at all. They wouldn't see the point of living if they knew death was around the corner.

No matter what they chose, time would always get wasted. Experiences wouldn't exist and regrets would be plentiful.

With that in mind, the older woman was also correct. All their cards were dealt—as she put it—and there was no changing it. Of course, it wasn't an actual deck of cards. That was an expression the Living World came up with.

In truth, every physical body had an internal clock from the moment the soul and physical form connect, known to them as being born. No one can see the clock, not even me. But it's there and you never know how much time you have left. The Living World celebrates birthdays, counting up in age. The fact was, the internal clock counted down. It was yet another misconception the Living World thought they were correct about. Regardless, the clock already decided how long the soul had left in their physical form the moment they're brought into the Living World. So, in a way, the cards are a decent analogy.

The gentleman broke me out of my thoughts as he sighed. He turned his attention to the shy man. "Don't worry about what she says. You're allowed to be scared and confused. I am, too."

"You are?" the young man asked. "How did you get here?"

I smiled, knowing this conversation headed in the right direction.

The older man leaned back in his chair, crossing one leg over the other and resting his hands in his lap. "I'm not sure," he said thoughtfully. "I went to sleep the other night and when I awoke, I was with them." He jutted a thumb toward me.

I nodded along, since the man told the truth. He didn't know how he died, but I did. He had a heart attack while sleeping and his physical form didn't react fast enough.

The gentleman continued with a frown, gazing at the floor. "I was getting married soon. She too got divorced before and, even though we were both hurt, we took a chance on each other. But now... well, I'll never know how that marriage was supposed to go."

The woman opened her mouth, but quickly shut it. I knew what she planned to say—they already knew the outcome of the marriage. It didn't exist. This man was always supposed to let go of his physical form at this time, regardless of him being engaged or not.

Instead, the woman looked at the two men with sympathetic eyes. "I guess not all of us can be so blessed. My ending is nothing to gloat about. I was sick in the hospital. My body and mind went long before I drew my last breath. My family eventually pulled the plug. They didn't know I could hear them, but I could. I heard the whole conversation. I listened to the silence when they caught their breaths between sobs. Maybe they felt guilty. Maybe it was relief. But I wanted to go," she said, perking up. "I wasn't living anymore and my vegetative state was a burden to my family. They shouldn't have had to spend months visiting me at that hospital."

But her family never pulled the plug. She had already died. What the woman remembered was her spirit watching over her family grieve over her empty physical form. She didn't seem at peace as much as she thought. She was so angry about the choices she had made in her life that she became blinded, unable to recognize how much her family loved her.

I knew this was my cue to speak.

"Leaving your physical form is never an easy journey. It doesn't matter if you're expecting it or if it's sudden," I said, looking at the two men. Then I turned to the woman. "It also doesn't matter if you're ready to leave your physical form or not."

"Every physical form," I continued, "has a certain amount of time in that body. It's not clear why some have a longer time than others. No matter how much time you have with your physical form, I believe you're meant to build relationships. Create memories and don't take that lifetime for granted. See what it offers because it has much more to offer than we realize."

"But we can't possibly figure it out, even if we live to be over 100 years old," the man replied.

I nodded. "You're right. That's why you're meant to discover as much as you can. It's the journey, not the destination."

"How do we know what to discover?" the young man questioned, sitting up in his chair again.

"What did you discover in your lifetime?" I asked, turning my full attention to him.

He thought for a moment. "Well... math is hard. Women don't make sense. Science explains everything and nothing at the same time. Even after living alone for two years, my mortgage payments still didn't make sense. I had my parents to support me, though. I spoke to my mother on the phone every night."

15

I smiled. "Then it sounds like you discovered hardships, but also that it's okay to ask for help. You discovered a parent's love."

His mouth gaped open. "Oh, *that's* what you meant by discovery."

"Again, there's more to life than we know," I repeated.

"I discovered love, too. Even when you can't love yourself, or you fall out of love with a special person, someone else will always be there to support you," the gentleman grinned.

The three of us turned to the woman, who lightly chuckled. "I guess you could say I discovered hardships as well."

"Did you overcome them?" the man asked.

"I suppose."

"What else?" the middle-aged man prompted knowingly.

She looked at him plainly. "I didn't have help or support like you two did. I struggled all my life and brought my family down with me."

"You mean the same family who sat by your bedside while you were in the hospital?" the young man pressed further, cracking a gentle smile.

The woman stared back at him, shocked at his words. "Yes, I... I suppose I discovered my own form of love. Despite everything, they held my hand until I let go."

The Clock turned red.

"Where do we go from here?" the young man asked.

The woman stood and headed for the door. "Now, I visit my family and help them in ways I couldn't before." She left without another word or ever looking back.

The gentleman stood, too. "I'm going to wander the Spirit World for a bit."

"Can I come, too?" the young man asked. "I don't know if I want to be alone."

"Of course."

The two of them exited side-by-side, leaving me behind.

Despite their lives in the Living World, they'd make friends and memories in the Afterlife. They'll help one another find their peace, visit old loved ones, and carry those old lives with them. Each life is a unique experience. Everyone learns the same lesson, but it's taught differently to all.

THE SECOND GROUP

I MADE A STEAMING cup of tea appear in front of the woman sitting across from me. I then created a coffee for myself. The burning sensation still felt good, even though the caffeine had zero effect on me. I still liked to believe it made a difference, for this session was one where I needed all my strength.

The spirit rested her head on the surface of the table, sobbing into the crook of her elbow. She had visited me twice before, so we skipped the introductions and headed right into the tears.

The first time she visited, the soul was in denial. She didn't think she should be here. It wasn't her time to go. It was the same spiel I had heard many times over from other spirits. Each time I had to explain about the internal clock. The moment a spirit is born to a physical form in the Living World, their internal clock ticks down. It didn't measure time in the way they understood it. It measured how much time they had left. No one can see it. No one knows it's there. And, if they knew of its presence, they wouldn't know how to read it.

Then, when she visited the Crossover Room a second time, she was angry. Really angry. At me.

I admit, out of the countless spirits I've aided, she takes the top spot to scare me most. And I've dealt with a lot of vengeful spirits before.

Like many before her, this spirit was angry she was here and not back in the Living World with her children and grandchildren. She was 73-years-old and her third grandchild had just been born. She couldn't believe the audacity I had to take her away from her family so soon.

The problem was, I couldn't control her illness. Again, it was up to their internal clock. Sometimes it lasted many years, for others it didn't. Even I didn't know the rhyme or reason behind it.

Another problem was that she believed me to be the bad guy since I took her away from her physical form. It's an old story I heard time and time again and, as the Grim Reaper, I had to grin and bear it.

A rumor started in the Living World that the Grim Reaper, me, caused death. But I had nothing to do with it. I was here to help and, no matter how many times I tried to explain that, I'd always be seen as the bad guy.

Spirits pleaded with me, argued with me, to release them back into the Living World. I wasn't keeping them here. If I could send them back to make them happy, I would. But that's not how it works. As much as I wanted to clear my name, it wasn't my job to convince the spirits of this. They'd eventually realize it, even though the Living World would never understand.

This woman wasn't much different from the others. She simply went through the typical stages of grief. Yes, spirits encountered grief much like they would if they grieved someone else in their physical form.

First denial, then anger, and now...

"PLEASE," she begged, head still on the table. She raised her fist, banging it. Luckily, it didn't make a sound.

Bargaining. The worst stage.

I could handle denial and, of course, acceptance. I could also deal with the yelling of anger and blubbering of depression. But bargaining? I was powerless to the spirits, who thought I held all the power within my scythe. Instead, my only weapon in this case was reassurance.

"Have a sip of tea," I coaxed.

She lifted her head enough for me to see the darkening of her eyes as she glared daggers into my soul. If I wasn't already dead, I would be now.

"It'll help you feel better," I said, gently pushing her cup closer to her.

She finally sat up in her chair, staring at the steaming cup. She held onto the mug with both hands, sniffling. Then she smiled a bit. "It's warm."

I nodded. Some of her physical form still lingered, so she could feel its warmth. Being our third session, this is the first time I've gotten her to acknowledge her beverage.

Suddenly, the glare returned. She arched a brow at me. "Is it poison?"

"No," I said, shaking my head. I wanted to remind her she was already dead, but figured that most likely wasn't the correct response.

The spirit brought the mug to her lips and tasted the tea. She sipped delicately before putting it back down on the table, wearing a face of disgust.

"You'll lose your taste buds overtime, which is why it tastes funny. For now, the effects of the tea will help you feel calm," I explained.

She sighed, her shoulders relaxing. In a gentle tone, she spoke again, looking at me with pleading eyes. "What can I do to fix this? My grandchildren need their grandmother. My daughter still needs her mother."

I frowned. "I'm sorry, but all I can do is help you feel comfortable here now. Once you get used to the Spirit World, there is a way to check in on those left in the Living World."

"I can speak to them?"

"Not exactly. You can leave subtle hints to let them know you're around."

She slouched in her seat, still clutching her warm mug. "But what can I *do* to go back?"

"Nothing," I replied. Blunt, but sometimes that was the only way to get through to them.

She slouched further in her chair, frowning so deep I thought her lips would fall off.

"Do you see that clock?" I pointed to The Clock on the wall in the room with us. I noticed it was already orange, which meant time ran out for this session already. "Every person has that inside themselves once they're born into the Living World. Yours turned red. That's why you're here."

The woman stared at The Clock, familiar with it from her previous sessions. Then she turned her curious gaze back to me. "Can't I change its batteries?"

"Batteries?"

"Can you recharge it?"

"What?"

"I *need* to go back to my kids!"

Sighing, I said, "I'm sorry, but that clock is human nature. It has nothing to do with me or with you. No one can reverse time or fast forward it. We can't pause it, no matter how much we want to. Once it turns red, that's it."

"But how was I supposed to know it would turn red soon...?" she sniffled, tears beginning to spill from her eyes now. It seemed the bargaining stage ended and depression began.

"No one knows when it's going to turn red," I stated reassuringly. "I don't even know when The Clock up there is going to turn. All I know is that it gives us the time we need."

"But how was I supposed to know how much time I had?" she questioned again.

As if on cue, The Clock turned red.

I knew she had more thoughts, and I had more to say to her as well. Since she exited the bargaining stage, maybe that was all we needed to accomplish during this session. I knew she'd be a suitable candidate for a group session if I could get her to agree.

Before dismissing her, I replied, "That's one of life's many mysteries."

***

"By the time I had gotten out of the army, I thought my life was over. I had nowhere to go. I had no home to go back to. Both my parents died while I was away, and I wasn't there to bury them. Their house got sold, too. I didn't know what to do."

I sipped my tea, listening intently. The elderly gentleman sitting across the table from me recounted his previous life in great detail. He told his story confidently, only stopping to sip his beverage. Even during the sad parts of his tale, he never stopped smiling.

I never preferred one spirit over another, but these kinds of sessions were some of my favorites. The stories were refreshing. No one was angry or yelling. Best of all, no one blamed me for their death.

The souls, like the man before me, were already at peace. Logically, they didn't need to be here in the Crossover Room. However, some of them enjoyed reminiscing about their life from the Living World. They were dead, but the memories were still very much alive.

I believed some thought they'd soon forget their previous life and wanted to ensure they told as many spirits as possible about what they did, said, and encountered in their physical form. Or maybe they were boasting about their story, proud of the life they lived.

"I almost arrived here about 35 years ago. Did you know that?" he asked.

I shook my head. I didn't know when anyone was going to show up to the Afterlife. Also, I didn't know anyone before they became spirits, either.

The old man sighed, though he still smiled. "It's true. I didn't see a will to live anymore. My parents were gone. My best friend from the army perished in the war. No siblings, no relatives that were close by. At least, not to my knowledge."

I drank my tea some more, his story similar to others I've heard before. Not only was he older, but he already had one foot in the grave due to his own hand—or mind. So, arriving in their spirit form because of other circumstances, and at a much later age, was a relief to them.

"I tried finding an apartment," he continued, sitting back in his chair. He looked at me as though we'd been friends for years. "I didn't have much money and, despite being a veteran, no one wanted to rent to me. I tried one place and when I told them my income, they tried denying me. But then, a woman appeared. She barged into the landlord's office, out of breath, apologizing to us for being late."

I grinned as he chuckled, lifting his shoulders into a shrug. "I didn't know who she was, but she pretended to know me, and I went along with it. You see, she wasn't able to afford any apartments in the area, either. She overheard some of our conversation and hatched a plan. We could combine our incomes and became roommates. She was around my age, so we thought it was a good idea. But, of course, we became much more than roommates."

His certainly was one of the more interesting stories I had heard. It was true how life threw odd events our way. One moment you're down on your luck and, suddenly, all it takes is one person to give you a chance, giving you the boost you need.

"Before I knew it, I had a family again," the man continued. "We weren't lovers, just friends. The best of friends. She had a wonderful family and lovely friends. I became part of those groups. Her family accepted me with warm hearts. I'll never forget it. I couldn't imagine what would have happened if she and I didn't get along."

"We may not know the reasoning behind these chains of events, and they can be good or bad, depending on your outlook. However, in that moment, you took a chance, and it made all the difference," I stated.

"I saw an opportunity, yes," he added. "I don't know what it was, but something was there and I took that chance without thinking. Our choices make a difference, big or small. We'll always ask the what-ifs, but we'll never know unless we act. We need to take those risks."

"You and that woman took a big risk," I agreed, nodding along.

The man tilted his head back and laughed. "The landlord did eventually figure us out. It didn't take long. But he didn't mind in the end because we were good tenants. Clean, kind to the neighbors, and quiet. Despite our money troubles, we were always on time with the rent."

He took a sip of his drink and then frowned. I furrowed my brows, confused at the sudden shift in emotion.

He bowed his head, cracking a small, sad smile. "She died three years ago. We had stopped living together long before then, of course. She met a wonderful man, married him, and created a beautiful family with him. A new family she still allowed me to be part of. I missed her dearly when she passed on. But I was happy to help her husband and children, even though they were all grown."

The Clock turned orange as the man looked back up at me. A genuine smile returned to his face.

"Thank you for listening to my story."

Holding up my drink as a toast, I bowed my head. "That's what I'm here for. I'm always happy to listen, and I'm pleased you lived such a wonderful life."

"I did lead an amazing life, didn't I?" he said, his tone drifting into a ponder.

Now The Clock turned red. I smiled, knowing this gentleman would be alright in the Spirit World.

He stood, as though he knew The Clock had dismissed him. "I can't wait to find my friend again in the Spirit World."

"Well, might I suggest paying a visit to the Living World?" I recommended. "I have a sneaking suspicion she won't be too far from her family."

His grin grew. "Even better! I'll get to see my family again."

***

"I always dreamed about moving away. I wanted to get away from my family for many reasons, but I never wanted it to get to the point I'd never speak or see them ever again." The soul sipped her coffee, sighing. She peered into the mug, frowning. "Not enough sugar, I think."

I explained to her she'd lose her taste overtime, though the woman didn't seem to hear me.

"I had dreams, you know?" she continued, putting her mug down on the table. She folded her hands together in her lap, looking at me. "Everyone says you shouldn't take life for granted. Anything can change in an instant, but you never think it'll happen to you."

I nodded, sipping my tea. I didn't taste mine at all, either, but I drank it because I liked the burning sensation on my tongue. The tingling allowed me to feel something. It had been so long, after all.

Her chuckle broke me out of my thoughts and it was then I realized she no longer looked at me, but outside the window beside us.

"You probably hear that speech a lot, huh?" she asked into the emptiness.

"No," I lied. "Every experience is unique. Whatever you have to say comes from your heart."

"What heart? Mine is no longer beating."

"That may be," I replied reassuringly, "but your heart is still part of you. Your heart carried your soul for 48 years, allowing you to feel, celebrate milestones, love, and experience all life offers. Now, your soul carries that heart. It may not beat anymore, but it holds many memories."

She smiled. It was a sad smile, but the smile was there all the same. Maybe I was helpful, maybe I wasn't. Maybe she tried being nice because what else could she do? She was here to stay. Whether she accepted that was up to her.

"You're right," she said, leaning back and relaxing her shoulders, "I experienced a lot in life, didn't I?"

"You absolutely did," I agreed. Although, I didn't know what she had experienced in life. This was our first time meeting and, so far, all she's talked about is how she wasn't ready to cross over to the other side.

It was a common side effect of separation. I had seen it many times over again. As soon as the soul separates from its physical form, I appear to help them cross over to the side. Most of the times, the spirit is confused. Sometimes angry, but mostly confused and sometimes somber.

Those are the emotions I'd expect to see, so it never bothered me. I sometimes feel sympathetic towards them. Some days, my caseload is filled to the brim with seemingly unexpected deaths. I can deal with anger and sadness, but when they're confused about why they've crossed over, I feel for them.

Occasionally, I'd have a case where the soul was already at peace. Those were easy. Once I helped a woman—103 years old—cross over. Her relief and joy were almost contagious.

The woman in the room with me now was not so lucky—in her late 40s, on her way to work in the rain, and got hit by a hydroplaning bus. She never stood a chance. Thankfully, death came instantly. Not that it makes it any easier, but if you're going to separate from your body, it's best if it's quick. If there's no chance of saving yourself, you might as well not be aware you ever had the option.

She buried her face in her hands. "Ugh, I met someone at the coffee shop just two days ago. I was supposed to call him. Not he's going to think I ghosted him."

She let go of her face, eyes wide. Sheepishly, her gaze cast over to me. "I mean... no pun intended, of course."

"Of course," I agreed indifferently.

"Was that offensive?"

"Not to me."

The woman breathed a sigh of relief, relaxing her shoulders once more.

The Clock turned orange, though I didn't know why. I didn't think we accomplished much in this session.

"It looks like we should begin wrapping things up," I said, nodding my head toward The Clock. I knew she could always come back. Maybe this was The Clock's way of telling me she'd be good for a group session—if The Clock could even tell such a thing.

The woman stared at The Clock. "I see. I'm sure you're very busy."

I didn't respond. The truth was, I was never busy and always busy at the same time. Many spirits left their physical forms every second, day and night. The bridge to cross over always filled. I either had to help the spirits along or I was here, talking to them about what to do next.

The souls waiting their turn often thought they were in limbo, making them quite panicky. It was another rumor set up by the Living World. If you were neither good nor bad, you'd end up in some sort of purgatory forever. But really, there was one of me and billions of them. I did my best but sometimes, they'd have to wait their turn.

"Do you have any final words?" I asked.

The spirit shook her head. The Clock turned red, which startled her. "Can I come back here?" she asked, turning her attention to me again.

"Yes, of course," I responded.

She stood, grinning sadly again. I watched her exit the Crossover Room, wondering why The Clock ended the session when we barely chatted.

Regardless, I knew I'd see her again. Maybe I'd invite her to a group session since she seemed hesitate to talk about anything at first.

I peered into her coffee mug. She barely drunk any of it, though that didn't surprise me. It was difficult to get used to the non-taste.

***

Once everyone sat at the table and had their drinks, I created a cup of coffee for myself. Sitting around me was an old army veteran, a 48-year-old woman, and a 73-year-old woman. The older lady sobbed into the table while the gentleman rubbed her back in gentle circles. The middle-aged woman watched with a brow raised, sipping her coffee.

"Would anyone like to start?" I opened the floor, hoping the older woman would speak her mind. Instead, she continued bawling. I don't even think she heard me.

The gentleman turned his gaze to me, still rubbing the lady's back. "Maybe this young woman would like to? If she can?"

I nodded, though I wasn't sure how we'd convince her.

She lifted her head, sniffling. "You think I'm... young?" she gazed at the man.

Apparently, that would do it.

I noticed the other woman roll her eyes as the gentleman smiled sweetly at the distraught spirit.

"Come on, that's enough. We're here and now it's time to move on," she said, groaning out of annoyance.

I frowned at her. "It's not that simple for most."

She sighed, leaning back in her seat. She crossed her arms together. "I know. I don't mean to be insensitive, but it's true. Can we go back to living our lives?"

"Unfortunately not."

"Exactly."

The older woman sat up, looking at the other lady. "Hey, I was sick. I shouldn't have died from that. The doctors should have made me better and I should be with my children and grandchildren right now. I'm too young to be here!"

The 48-year-old leaned closer, pointing to herself, glaring at the lady. "And *I'm* not too young to be here? I'm younger than you and I got hit by a bus!"

The gentleman held up both his hands, attempting to silence the two ladies. "I'm sorry to hear that," he said to the younger one. "We never know where life will take us."

"To hell, apparently," she scoffed with an eye roll.

Before I could reply, the man spoke up again.

"We're not in hell," he corrected. "We're in the Afterlife. Our lives are over, this is what comes after. It's natural."

I nodded in agreement, putting those words in my back pocket for later.

It was natural. Dying was the next stage of life, despite what most people believed. In the Living World, death is explained as the end, but it's just another beginning. For those who believe in the Afterlife are afraid of what they'll lose from their current physical form. It's still an end, even though they're still connected to that part of them.

"But why did I have to come here when my next grand baby was just born?" the older woman questioned, her face twisting in preparation to sob once more.

The other woman peered sadly into her tea. "I was supposed to go on a date soon. At least, I think so. I met someone and I don't know if it was going anywhere."

The gentleman cast a smile at the two ladies. "I'm sorry to hear your lives cut seemingly short when something good was about to happen. But those can't be the only good things that happened to you. Life has no end, so if you didn't arrive at the Afterlife now, you probably would have gotten here before the next big thing happened."

The middle-aged woman nodded along. "I guess you're right. In a way, it's a good thing I'm here now before I found out what could have been with that guy."

"It could have been heartbreak or it could have been happily ever after. Instead of mulling over the unknown, be grateful for the things that happened in your life," the man explained.

The older woman sat up in her chair. "But what good can come from knowing my grand baby won't know her grandmother?"

"You arrived after she was born?" he asked.

She nodded.

"You got to meet her? Hold her?"

The woman lifted her chin, grinning. "Yes, I did. She was beautiful. So peaceful and innocent."

I couldn't help but smile at the memory, and it wasn't even mine. I noticed the other woman smiled, too.

"Then it's good you got to meet her. She won't remember, but she'll see pictures of you holding her as she grows. Your children and other grandchildren will tell her all about you," the gentleman explained.

Her shoulder finally relaxed. "I supposed that's true. She'll get to know me through memories the rest of my family has of me."

"And," I added, "you can visit them as a spirit whenever you want. You can drop subtle hints to let them know you're alright."

She smiled at me, resting back against her chair. She held her teacup in her lap; her gaze now wandering. "Do you think," she began, "my husband is here, too? He passed two years ago."

"Of course," I replied.

She melted into her chair, closing her eyes peacefully.

The Clock was still green. I knew the gentleman had already accepted being here, which was why I asked him to come to this group session. Both women struggled, and he was a strong backup for me—although I thought he did a better job than I did.

So, I turned my attention to the other woman. She downed her coffee like it was a shot of alcohol before putting it back onto the table with vigor.

"What about you?" the gentleman asked before I had a chance to.

She glanced up, noticing all three of us staring at her. She shrugged, tearing her gaze away, embarrassed. "I don't know. I didn't do much. Wasn't married, didn't have kids. Nothing. I might have met the one in that coffee shop, but now I'll never know."

"You must have been busy with other things in life," the gentleman coaxed. "What sort of things did you accomplish?"

"Accomplish?" she questioned with a chuckle. "It's not like I defended my country." She pointed to him for emphasis.

The gentleman pointed to the 73-year-old. "Neither did she."

The other woman responded quick. "I didn't get married and start a family or anything."

27

"Did you want to?" I asked.

The lady hesitated, pondering my question. Finally, she shook her head. "No, I don't think so. But it would have been nice to have someone to grow old with. You know... if I had the chance to grow old, I mean."

"That sounds reasonable," I replied. "But you must have focused on something else in your lifetime. What was it?"

She shrugged. "All I did was work."

"What did you do for work?"

"I sold cars."

"That's a respectable job," the gentleman piped up.

She snorted, crossing her arms. "It's not world-changing or anything."

"Do you think you need to change the world to live?" I inquired.

She cocked her head to the side in confusion. Even the other two souls in the room stared quizzically at me.

"Do you think your life mattered any less because you didn't have a world-changing job?" I reworded my question.

"I guess not," she shrugged, "but it's not like I cured world hunger or anything."

"I didn't do that, either," the older woman replied.

"But you created life," she remarked. She looked at the gentleman. "You defended your country." She slumped back into her chair, huffing. "I sold air pollution."

"May I ask what world-changing means?" I questioned.

She arched a brow at me. "It means to change the world."

"What does world-changing mean *to you?*"

She narrowed her eyes, more confused than before. She looked at the other two spirits, though they weren't about to help her. It seemed I had puzzled them, too, so they opted to stay out of the conversation for now. I remained silent, staring at her, waiting for her answer.

Finally, she spoke up. "World-changing means to... you know, change the world. Get rid of hunger, homelessness, war... defend your country, keep the population going..."

And there she was, comparing herself to the other spirits again. She continued listing off things others have done in the past, things she learned in history class. I nodded along, allowing her to get it out of her system, but she was wrong about it all.

Sure, those people made a mark on the world. Many people made a difference, but to who? Some people made it into history textbooks or had books written about them and their work. Others would appear on the news only to be forgotten the following week or even the next day.

It was another common misconception the Living World created. Humans overthink and look at the bigger picture. Many want to "change the world" but few do because they define "world-changing" literally.

"How would you solve homelessness?" I asked, interrupting her train of thought.

The middle-aged spirit paused for a minute. "I never really thought about it. Maybe build a cheap hotel for people to move into?"

"Everywhere?"

She didn't answer. She only looked at me with more confusion.

"Getting rid of homelessness around the world is a big feat. Do you know the exact number of homeless people around the entire world?" I questioned.

She remained speechless. All of them were.

"Building a hotel is a great idea for those to find shelter, build a community together, and have a legal address to find a job. But how many people can fit into one hotel? Out of the many homeless people, how many would you actually help with just one hotel?"

The spirit bit her lip. "Uh, I guess I'd build more than one?"

"Where?"

"Anywhere?"

"How are you going to build a hotel for the homeless on the other side of the world?"

She cast a glance at the other two spirits, silently pleading for aid, no doubt. When neither of them acknowledged her, she turned her attention back to me, tossing her hands in the air in surrender. "Alright, you've lost me."

"If you could build only one hotel to shelter the homeless, would you do it?" I asked gently.

"Of course."

"Is that considered world-changing?"

"No, because it's only a small area," she replied.

"But you said you'd still do it for that one area," I pressed.

"Yes. Something is better than nothing. Even if I can't help everyone, I can at least help someone. And maybe someone else will think it's a great idea and build a similar hotel for their area," She explained.

"Exactly," I grinned. "You don't need to do something great. Something memorable. All you need to do is inspire. Inspire one person to inspire another. Inspire a group of people and those individuals will branch out to inspire others. Inspiration creates a domino effect."

She chuckled. "That's good and all, but I didn't actually create a hotel for the homeless."

"Right, you sold cars to people," I stated.

The spirit stared at me as if I were losing it.

I looked at the gentleman. "Your friend inspired you to keep going when no one else wanted to give you a chance." I turned my gaze to the other woman. "And you inspired your family by caring for them right until your last moments." I then turned to the 48-year-old. "And you inspired others by giving them a car."

She snickered in disbelief. "I wouldn't call that inspirational."

"No, I see what they're saying," the gentleman piped up. "I'm sure you gave many people their first car, allowing them the freedom to bring themselves to school, work, their friend's house, whatever."

"And what about those people that had trouble taking their driver's test? Or they spent years saving up for the right car?" the older woman chimed in. "It might not sound like a lot to you, but I'm sure the people you sold cars to remember you."

"They drive by the dealership you worked at and say they got their car there from you," the gentleman added.

"When others ask for recommendations, they'll say I got my car from this dealership and spoke to a nice young lady about it," the other woman continued.

The middle-aged spirit cracked a smile. She gazed down at the floor sheepishly. "I met some wonderful customers. The car business is tricky because everyone assumes you're scamming them. Some of my co-workers had difficult customers, but I rarely did. I guess I was good at my job, huh?"

"You don't need to change the entire world to make a difference," I said. "You still mattered, and your role in society was important. You liked your job, I assume?"

She nodded with a genuine smile on her face.

I looked at the gentleman. "Were you happy with your life?"

"I'm happy with my struggles and how I overcame them," he said, nodding along. "It made me who I am."

I grinned, turning to the other spirit. "Were you happy with your life?"

She smiled proudly. "I had a supportive family growing up and created a beautiful, loving family in my later years. I was very content with my life."

I turned my attention back to the other woman. "And were you happy with your life?"

She hesitated, but finally nodded in agreement. "You know what? Yeah. I had a good job and lived in a good home with a few fun roommates. We all got along and became family."

"It sounds like you all lived full lives, vastly different from one another, but they were all worth living," I explained. "You might not have changed the world, but you made a difference to others, and that may mean the world to them."

THE THIRD GROUP

"So, THIS IS THE bad place?"

"No."

"We're not down below?"

I blinked at the man sitting across from me at the table. Shaking my head, I said, "the Afterlife doesn't work that way."

He frowned, tilting his head in confusion. "But I thought...?"

"You thought whatever you were raised to believe, but the truth is, the living doesn't know what happens when you cross over," I explained.

The man froze, and for a moment, I thought he malfunctioned. I had a spirit do that once—they were so excited to meet the god they believed in and when I burst their bubble...

"Wow, what a relief!" the man threw himself back, nearly knocking his chair over, belly laughing.

Oh. He was one of those.

The spirit laughed for a while. I sat, sipping my tea, calmly.

I had seen these kinds of spirits before, too. Many were excited to meet the deity they believed throughout their time in the Living World, while others were afraid. Usually, it was because they had done some questionable things during their lifetime.

"I assumed with you being the Grim Reaper and all, everything else would be true," he said.

I hid my frustration behind a sip of my beverage. I didn't know many living beings who actually believed the Grim Reaper was real. Many folks viewed me as a myth of some sort. Some believed I was death itself, not an actual being. The living believed in many gods and devils before they believed in me.

"So, what do I do now that there's no up or down?" the spirit asked, finally controlling his laughter.

"You can do whatever you want. Many spirits like to head back to the Living World. They'll visit and aid their loved ones," I explained.

He scoffed, dismissively waving his hand.

"Or," I continued, "other spirits remain here, resting. They may help other spirits who are still figuring things out."

He nodded along, but his gaze was elsewhere. There was nothing to look at, but he clearly had his mind on other things. I took another sip of my tea, deciding to let him carry the conversation. I wasn't sure how to help this guy, if he even needed help. He was so relieved to know the bad place wasn't real; I think that alone helped him find peace.

Yet, The Clock remained green.

"Do I have to help other spirits if I stay here?" he questioned.

"You don't need to interact with anyone if you don't want to," I stated.

He grinned, leaning back in his chair. He crossed his legs, folding his hands together behind his head. "Wow, this is so cool."

I sipped my tea some more. This spirit was so beside himself that he wasn't in a bad place. I couldn't help but wonder why he thought he'd end up there. My curiosity piqued, but I didn't want to ask. It wasn't my business. My job was to help him find peace. However, with The Clock still green, I knew something bugged him underneath his excitement. It might have been deep under the excitement, but there was more to this man, for sure.

"Do you know everything about those who die?" he asked suddenly, uncrossing his legs and leaning forward. He eyed me intensely.

I shook my head. All I knew was how they died. I didn't even know their names.

He smirked. "So, you don't know anything about me?"

"If there's something you'd like to share, you're more than welcome," I invited with an even tone.

"And I can stay here no matter what?"

"There's nowhere else for you to go."

I knew where this conversation headed. I had encountered spirits like him before. They did questionable things in the Living World and assumed they'd be damned for all eternity. As soon as they realize that's not the case, they're overwhelmed with arrogant relief.

"I killed a man," he explained, unprompted. He gazed into his beverage. "Two, actually."

I had a hard time reading his expression. It was plain. Was it from guilt? Disbelief he ever did such a thing?

"I served some time for the first murder," he continued. "It was an accident. Involuntary manslaughter or something like that. I didn't have to serve long because I had a smart lawyer." He grinned. "I didn't serve any time for the second murder. That would have been worse because that one was on purpose."

I remained silent. He couldn't do any harm in the Spirit World, but I didn't want to hear about his supposed triumphs in the Living World. My job was to help those who have crossed over find peace and give them a space to relive fond memories from their time in the Living World. However, some of these sessions were tougher than others because I had to remain impartial. I didn't always agree with the actions of a spirit, but it wasn't my place to do anything about it. I was here to listen, and that's what I did.

"They never found the body," he continued, relaxing his shoulders. He looked off into the distance. "As far as the police are concerned, it's a missing person's case. They must know the dude is dead by now; it was two years ago. But without a body..." he chuckled, clicking his tongue. "Not that it matters now. I'm dead. Even if they figure out it was me, they can't touch me here." He laughed straight from his gut again.

As the laughter faded, he frowned. "I died from a drunk driver. That's how I killed the first guy. I guess that's what you'd call karma, huh?"

I nodded, although I thought karma was too kind to him. I glanced at The Clock and it remained green. Some sessions seemed to last longer than others.

Then he sighed, the smile completely wiped from his face. "My wife recently found out about my affair, too."

Oh, there's more.

"So, I'm sure she's happy I'm dead. My mistress was the one who told her, so I'm sure she won't come to my funeral, either." He looked out into the void through the window. "If I get a funeral, that is. I never took my mother's advice to get a will and get my affairs in order."

Just as I detected a hint of remorse, he turned to wink at me with a smirk. "Unless I hid something from my wife or mistress, of course."

I didn't find the pun amusing.

When I didn't react, he continued. "I committed fraud at my work, too. Blamed the new guy. He got fired immediately, and they never figured out the truth. Poor guy ended up with a record. Took him years to get a new job."

He looked at me, a serious expression finally written on his face. "I wasn't a good guy, was I?"

"That's not for me to say," I responded. It was the truth. Even though I didn't agree with the things he told me, that didn't give me the authority to judge who he was when he was alive.

After all, people aren't born that way. In many cases, the good deeds outweighed the bad. Everyone made mistakes and got on the wrong path at some point in their lifetime. What mattered was that they found their way back to the right one.

He chuckled, crossing his arms. "Nah, I know I was a good guy. Sure, I did questionable things. But I only did what I had to do in the moment. I needed to protect myself, and that's what I did. There's nothing wrong with that."

I hid a smile. So, there was a hint of remorse. The only time spirits justified their actions was when they felt guilty about those actions. They sought the approval of others to make themselves feel better about what they did.

What the circumstances were for him to commit homicide, I wasn't sure, but I let him talk through his thoughts.

"It's not my fault the other people dealt with the consequences of my actions. They should have protected themselves better," he continued, grasping at straws now.

"Maybe they didn't have the resources to protect themselves against your actions," I stated. "Not everyone has friends, family, or the will to back themselves up."

He stared at me, quizzically. I didn't give him the chance to respond.

"That's one of the many reasons there are billions of living beings inhabiting the Living World at once. You push each other down, but you pick one another up again. You make mistakes, but learn from them. Together, you discover love, go through many experiences, and make memories. Not all of them are happy, but you do it together. You're never alone."

He hesitated, his mouth gaped open in shock. But then closed it, casting me a sad smile. "I don't argue with you, of course," he said, his tone gentle, "but I am alone. I was alone then and I am now. I did the things I did to protect myself because no one else would."

"Did you give them a chance to?" I asked.

He raised a brow, puzzled.

"Do you really believe your wife wouldn't have been there for you? Instead, you hid behind a mistress. You made a mistake at work and instead of working through it with your boss, you hid behind the new guy."

He sighed, another chuckle escaping his lips. "Alright, so you got me there. But what else was I supposed to do? Trust isn't easy to come by, so I got a mistress before my wife had the chance to leave me. Righting wrongs isn't simple, either. It takes work and effort. I didn't know how to fix my mistakes."

"You ask for help from your loved ones," I stated.

The spirit eyed me for a moment. "What loved ones? I lost them the moment I stepped off the beaten path."

"There's always someone willing to lend a hand."

"Not for me."

"I'm sure that's not true."

He shook his head. "It is. Would you go back to your husband after you dealt with the terrible publicity of them driving drunk and killing someone only for them to have an affair with the lawyer that got them an easy sentence? Would you help the guy who admits to fraud and letting some poor innocent man take the fall for it when he was fresh out of college, top of his class? And would you ever help that same man hide a body?"

I didn't answer. For the first time, I saw the remorse in his gaze. I noticed guilt buried deep beneath the layer of relief. Finally, I saw a man who recognized his selfish choices.

"You talk about discovering love. I had that once. I destroyed it," he continued, speaking softly. "You talk about experiences. I ruined people's lives, even taking some away. You talk about making memories with people. But the problem is, no two people make the same memory. I have a happy memory of keeping my job, but for the new guy? That's a memory filled with anger, confusion, shame."

Everyone was born with innocence and had good in them. Sometimes they needed help to find it again. However, he rendered me speechless. Before I could articulate a response, he stood, ready to dismiss himself.

"It's a shame there is no bad place," he said, looking around the empty space, "because that's where I belong. That's what I deserve."

The Clock turned the red at his words, and he left without looking back.

***

"It was an odd feeling. I felt lost. Incomplete, almost. But I didn't know why. As far as I was concerned, life continued on normally. But I was living in the past, completely unaware."

I nodded along, listening to the elderly woman go through the motions of her memory. She fought an unknown war with her mind for years before passing. She had dementia and, when she crossed over to the Afterlife, all her memories were here waiting for her.

"I lived a good life. I had three children, eight grandchildren, and two great-grandchildren. Isn't that something?" she said, smiling. She peered into her coffee mug, taking a sip and breathing a sigh of happiness. "This is so good. Even when I couldn't remember things, I still loved my coffee. My daughter always brought me a cup at my new home. They had to put me somewhere, you know. I couldn't take care of myself anymore and it got to be too much for my kids." She frowned.

"Does that bother you?" I asked.

She shook her head. "They did what was best for them and for me. They still visited me often. I got coffee. I met new people, even though I didn't know who they were. I liked them well enough. I had my own room."

I grinned, happy for her. There were times spirits came to me upset, believing their family gave up on them. But that was never the case. They simply couldn't see it from a different perspective.

"But why did this happen to me?" she asked, willing me to share the answer.

Unfortunately, I didn't have the answer for her. "The mind works in mysterious ways. I can't explain why you succumbed to dementia. There doesn't seem to be a rhyme or reason to it, but you were lucky enough to have your family's love and support through it all. Even if you weren't aware of it."

She smiled again, taking another sip of her beverage. "I guess I did something right along the way. But I can't imagine the pain I put them through. All I wanted to do was go home. They took me on so many car rides, but I didn't know where I was going. I just wanted to see my mom again."

"You can certainly do that now," I said. "I'm sure your mother is around here somewhere."

"And my husband?" she asked hopefully. "He died before me. They took me to his funeral to say goodbye, but... I didn't recognize him."

The Clock turned orange. I felt we had just started, but this woman was already accepting her peace. I believe her relief from remembering her life was peace enough.

"Your husband is here, too," I stated.

She stood as The Clock turned red. "I need to find him. I wasn't there when he had his health issues. He had to go through that alone. Well, my kids helped him, but you know."

"I'm sure he understands," I explained.

She grinned. "But I get to tell him I love him and actually remember why I do."

***

"But I didn't finish everything I wanted to."

I nodded along, sipping my tea. This soul spoke a lot about the many things she wanted to do during her lifetime, but never got the chance to. I let her talk through her thoughts, going through the motions of paying attention, nodding, and only chiming in when needed.

"I was going to try cross-stitching. I bought all the materials for it. It's in my closet. And what about my crochet projects? I was in the middle of making something for my niece and nephew. Oh, and candle making, too! That seemed like fun." She looked at me with desperation in her eyes. "Am I able to do any of that here?"

"We have everything you need here," I said.

She leaned back, sighing in relief.

"I should emphasize that we have everything you need, not want," I clarified.

She furrowed her brows in confusion.

"Once you cross over into the Spirit World, there isn't much you need to think about from the Living World. Unless, of course, you want to visit your loved ones again. If you have unfinished business, then there will be a way for you to complete that business if you wish," I explained further.

She blinked at me and I wasn't sure if my words sunk in. She leaned over the table, her curious gaze burning into me.

"My business being my crochet projects?"

"Most likely not."

She slumped back in her seat, pouting.

I didn't have the heart to tell her she'd lose her senses. Overtime, her soul would become so transparent, her sense of touch would diminish. Souls could touch, taste, and smell when needed. Otherwise, they were numb.

It's why I offered a warm beverage during these sessions. Warm beverages are a universal comfort. Not to mention, new souls have their body temperatures drop rapidly. Even if the spirits didn't understand the meaning behind it, the warm cup was a win-win all around.

"But if I really *need* to finish that crochet project, I can do it here? How will I get it to my niece and nephew?" she asked, scratching the top of her head.

"You don't," I replied bluntly. "But you can interact with things in the Living World to give subtle hints."

"Like a crochet doll?"

"You can't make things appear."

She huffed.

"You can whisper in their ear," I suggested. "Or move small objects slightly, put them in a different spot. You can create scents that'll make them think of you. Anything that's subtle enough to let them know you're still here."

She leaned forward again, taking in my words. "But what if they don't listen?"

"Sometimes they won't," I stated, shrugging. "It may take time or they might never notice. Alternatively, they might look and find all the signs. Not everyone will see or understand, but that's okay. Being in the Living World is a huge responsibility and can be stressful. Most living beings don't look for a sign until they're in desperate need of comfort."

The woman chuckled. "I only prayed when I needed something."

"Exactly." It was all too common.

She frowned, looking me in the eye once more. "You know why I'm so concerned about my art projects? I never finished anything I started. Once I got too far into a project, a job, a relationship... I don't know, I just had to shut it down right away."

The spirit looked around the emptiness before settling her gaze on The Clock, which glowed a deep green. "Now I'm here. I've never been married, never got the chance to make my own family. My sisters and brother got married and had children, though I rarely saw them. I was too embarrassed, I think, always being the single aunt at holiday gatherings, only tagging along because I had no family of my own. My parents died a long time ago and my siblings moved far away to be with their partners. I was alone. No friends, either. They all moved or wanted to go on big adventures. I wanted to join them; really, I did. But something always held me back, and now... well, now it's too late."

She smiled at me again, her expression bittersweet. "I didn't want to buy gifts this year for holidays or birthdays. I wanted to make them. But I guess I wasn't really doing it out of the goodness of my heart... I wanted to prove to myself I could finish something."

"I think there's more to it," I replied. "If you really did only do it for yourself, you wouldn't have put in so much effort. You wouldn't be so concerned about it now."

"No," she disagreed, "I put in the effort for myself, not for them."

"Because the effort needed to be for you and not for them," I stated. When she looked at me quizzically, I elaborated.

"You recognized something about yourself you wanted to change. You didn't want to change it for yourself, but for others instead. Otherwise, you wouldn't have noticed that change was needed. So, you created handmade projects for those you cared about to show them that, even though you don't go on those adventures with them, you still think about it."

"Whoa," the spirit let out a breath. "I guess I didn't realize."

"No one is supposed to realize everything about themselves. You need to go through the motions. Trust your instincts and your heart."

She finally picked up her tea, gulping it down. When she placed it back on the table, she stared back at The Clock, noticing it turned orange.

"I guess I accomplished some things," she said thoughtfully. "I job-hopped a lot, but I learned a lot of skills that way. I didn't make a family of my own, but my siblings included me as much as they could. My friends did, too, even though I didn't see them too often."

She turned her attention back to me, chuckling politely. "I was afraid to live and now there's no going back, huh?"

"Unfortunately, it's pretty common," I stated. "Everyone lives their life once, and no one takes it seriously until it's too late. However, you can still go on those adventures. You won't be there with them physically and they may not always know you're there, but you can still have the experience."

She hummed, deep in thought. "So, even though I'm in the Afterlife, I can still go to the Living World?"

"Yes. You can also find other souls here and make new friends."

"Really? I can do that?"

"Of course. You can go back and forth between here and the Living World however often you want."

She grinned, and it was the first time I'd seen her genuinely smile. Whatever regrets she had at the start of this session were gone now. She realized a new purpose for herself, even though she'd have to interact with her family in a much different way.

***

The next group sat in the Crossover Room. As I stared at the three souls sitting around the table with me, I realized something. They all—oddly enough—looked to be at peace already.

The elderly woman hummed happily into her coffee cup. The younger woman sat back in her chair, twiddling her thumbs, gazing mindlessly out the window. Finally, the man bopped his knees to some inaudible beat, his gaze wandering the room.

Or maybe it wasn't peace. Maybe it was nerves?

"Would anyone like to begin the conversation?" I broke the silence.

"What do you want to talk about?" the young lady asked, peeling her gaze away from the window.

I shrugged. "Anything you want to."

"I already talked to you. I don't have anything to say," the man stated, finally resting his knee. He slouched down in his chair, crossing one leg over the other.

"But you haven't met these two ladies," I retorted, gesturing to the two women.

The older one looked up from her coffee, grinning at us. I didn't think she heard the conversation, but just noticed we spoke about her. The other woman turned away, unresponsive.

"Am I supposed to be friends with them?" the man questioned, giving both women a dirty look.

"Not if you don't want to, but—"

"We've already had this conversation," he interrupted, standing from the table. "I'm not looking to go back to the Living World, so what am I doing here?"

I sighed. He couldn't leave the room. Not while The Clock remained green. Even if he tried to leave, he would wander this empty space for a long time before realizing the table was still a few feet away from him.

He was here because he agreed to be here. I asked him to join the group to learn from the other spirits. I didn't think he'd agree, so one can imagine my shock when he did. No one forced him to come back here. He was genuinely interested in what this group session would be about. Now that he was here, he clearly had second thoughts.

"Did you say you don't want to go back to the Living World?" the younger woman inquired, her attention suddenly on him with wide eyes.

He shook his head, staring at her, confused.

"Why?"

"Why does it matter?" he snapped.

"He must not have been happy with his life," the older woman remarked, sipping her coffee.

"Hey," the man glared at her, "you don't know anything about my life."

"I didn't know anything about mine, either," she stated.

He furrowed his brows before turning to me. He jutted a thumb at her as though silently asking if she was crazy.

I suppressed a chuckle.

The elderly woman explained. "I would give anything to go back and tell my family I love them. I want to tell them that and mean it. To know who I'm talking to and why. But I know if I went back, nothing would change. I still wouldn't remember who they are. All I can do is stay here and watch over them. They'll know I'm with them. They'll remember."

I grinned at her words. She found her peace quickly when she arrived here. Dementia held her mind hostage for years before arriving in the Spirit World. When she got here and remembered everything, her relief was overwhelming.

The younger woman frowned at a sudden realization. "You're right," she murmured. "Nothing would change if I went back. I still wouldn't finish anything I started."

"You made changes, slowly but surely," I said, comforting her. "It's who you are, but that doesn't mean you wouldn't improve if you wanted."

She cast me a sad smile, thankful for the kind words, though I didn't think she believed them.

The man scoffed, stealing my attention away. "You mean to tell me that if I went back, I wouldn't be able to turn my life around?"

"Would you want to?" I asked.

He stared at me for another moment before turning his gaze abruptly away.

"Every choice we make is different from what someone else would do. That's part of what makes your life unique. You're not supposed to agree with every decision you've made in your lifetime. Otherwise, your life would be perfect and there's no such thing. You're supposed to make mistakes and learn from them... or not," I explained. "If you didn't make choices, if you didn't make mistakes, then you wouldn't be living your life."

The room filled with silence. The elderly woman nodded her head in agreement, her grin disappearing into her coffee cup, while the young lady stared intensely at me, drinking in every word.

But then the man broke the silence, hands on his hips. "So, you're validating my choices, then?"

"Only you can judge yourself," I responded.

He groaned, sitting down in his chair once more. "I guess we live once and then have to deal with it, huh?"

The younger woman grunted, leaning back into her seat. "That one life for me is filled with regret. I didn't amount to anything in my life."

"Regret is knowledge," I interjected. "You must have learned something along the way if you recognize you did something you didn't want to. Not that what you did or didn't do was wrong, of course. You made the choice you thought was right. That was best for you at the time."

"See, the choices I made were right for me," the man said.

I didn't look at him. I kept a steady gaze on the ladies, though the elderly woman seemed to have already checked out of this conversation.

"What do I do now?" the young lady asked.

"You can help others find their potential," I encouraged.

The Clock turned orange as she stood. "Through that, I'll find my potential. Even though I rarely completed anything I started when I was alive, that doesn't mean I can't do so now. And the best part is I can take my time with it."

It was an interesting perspective, to say the least. Normally, when spirits came to the Afterlife, they wanted to right all their wrongs immediately. Once they discovered what they can do, they do everything at once—or try to, anyway. Much like her life when she was alive, this woman still planned on taking her time to do what she wanted. There was nothing wrong with that, of course, especially now that she seemed to have all the time in the world.

"Can I go now?" the elderly woman piped up.

The Clock hadn't dismissed us yet, but it was close. We waited for one more spirit to have an epiphany about their situation. Before I could respond to her, the man spoke up.

He walked away from the table, standing beside the window. "I didn't amount to much in my life. I didn't help others, only myself. I made the right choices at the time because they were right for me. I only ever thought about myself. Even then, it was always to get myself out of a jam. How did I get like that?" he looked over his shoulder at me.

"I don't know," I said, shrugging. I didn't know what his life was like. I didn't know anything about him other than what he had told me in his previous session. Even if I had that knowledge, he needed to come to his own conclusions.

"There is no bad place because we're all meant for the same destiny," he stated. "No matter how you lived your life, you can still learn from your mistake from beyond and help guide others. Now that we're in the Afterlife, we have more knowledge than ever. Whatever we learned from living, what we did or didn't do, and using what we know now, we can help those in the Living World. I wasn't a good guy then, but I can be now."

He stepped away from the window, standing over me. "Is that why we're here?"

The Clock turned red.

The souls dismissed, and I remained pondering his question alone.

THE FOURTH GROUP

"Fascinating."

I watched the soul pace the room, looking around. Although there was nothing to see. The only real beings in this room were myself and the other spirit. Even the table was an illusion, along with the beverages, but they were as real as I could muster.

"Really fascinating."

Aside from us, the only other lively thing in the room was The Clock. It wasn't alive, though it served an important purpose. Its light brightened the room a bit, which was comforting for some souls.

"This is really fascinating."

I furrowed my brows, watching the soul roam the empty area. Was that all she could think to say?

But then she stopped moving. She looked over her shoulder at me, smiling. "I never would have imagined this place."

Lots of people imagined black voids. It wasn't hard to do. Not everyone remembered their dreams, either, as though they slept in a black pit within their mind.

"The clock is a pleasant touch, I suppose. Is it possible to get any more light in here?" she roamed the room again, pointing to The Clock before gesturing to the entire space.

I shook my head, though she wasn't looking at me.

"I think maybe some curtains on the window would help tie this room together a bit more. Maybe a couch over there?"

I couldn't get a good read on this spirit. Was she excited to be in the Afterlife? Why did she want to decorate the place? Was it out of nerves? Maybe she tried buttering me up, so I'd let her go back to the Living World.

"Would you like to sit down and drink your tea?" I prompted, pointing to the chair across from me.

Immediately, she sauntered to the table and sat down. She picked up her teacup, smelling it before taking a sip. "This tastes good, too."

Ah, she definitely tried buttering me up.

"Thank you." It was all I could think to say. She gave no signs of distress or confusion. The soul seemed like she didn't mind being here. There was something off about her, though I couldn't figure out what.

"I'm assuming this is where the bad people go?" she finally inquired about the Spirit World.

I couldn't help but smirk. Now I understood. She thought decorating the place would make her feel better about being in this supposed bad place.

"No," I answered plainly. "There is one Spirit World—that's here—and it's where all souls go when they depart the Living World."

She hummed to herself, taking another sip of tea. She then stood, cup in hand, and wandered the room, her gaze dancing over the darkness.

I observed her. I had never seen this form of denial before. It was as though she was aware she was dead, yet I got the feeling she thought this was all a dream. Almost like she thought she'd wake up at any moment. Or maybe her pacing was her subtle way of looking for a way out.

"Can I do anything I want to this room?" she asked.

"No, this is the Crossover Room. I meet here with newly departed souls who need to talk things out."

"Oh," she said. Was that relief in her tone? She moseyed back to the table, sitting. She chuckled, gripping her mug tight. "I thought this was my bedroom."

Now it all made sense.

"Do I have a bedroom here?" she questioned.

"You don't need a bedroom here," I said, shaking my head. "There's no need for you to sleep."

"Oh."

"Now that you're a spirit, you won't need to eat, drink, sleep, or do much of anything you did when you were alive. You can meet other spirits and befriend them. Many spirits go back to the Living World for their loved ones," I explained.

She sat taller. "I can do that?"

"You can."

"Like a second chance?"

I hesitated. "Second chance for what?"

"Life."

"No."

She frowned, her shoulders dropping again.

"You don't go back to the Living World to *live*," I clarified. "But you can go back as a spirit to watch over your loved ones. No one will hear or see you, but you can drop subtle hints to let them know you're there."

Her eyebrows arched up, suddenly intrigued. "So," she said, "I can be a ghost?"

"Yes," I replied. Although, she technically already was a ghost, but I figured I'd let her think what she wanted for now.

"That's pretty cool!" she grinned, leaning back in her chair.

I pressed my lips into a smile. Most souls reacted in one of two ways when being reminded they're dead: excited or freaked out; there was no in between. Both emotions were hard to deal with because the ones who freaked out always tried bargaining with me. The thought of being an apparition scared them.

On the other hand, the excited ones...

"Can I walk through walls and stuff?" she asked.

I nodded.

She fist-pumped the air, giggling.

The excited ones immediately planned what they wanted to accomplish as ghosts. They thought about all the things they could do now they weren't able to when they were alive. Walking through walls was a popular one and so was eavesdropping on conversations.

It was a curse to some, but a silver lining to others.

She finished her tea, peering into her cup. I asked if she wanted a refill, though she shook her head.

"I can barely taste it," she said, looking up at me with concern on her face.

"That'll happen. Now that you're a spirit, you'll lose some of your senses overtime. Taste, touch, and smell will all be gone."

She relaxed her shoulders, crinkling her nose. "I won't be able to smell?" she asked in a confused tone.

"No," I stated.

"But if I can still use my eyes and ears, why can't I use my nose?"

"I agree it's a weird one to lose, but I don't make the rules."

"Why won't I be able to taste anything?"

"You don't get hungry. There's no need to eat as a spirit."

"But what about touching things?"

"Solid beings can't walk through walls," I clarified.

She nodded along, satisfied with that answer.

Sure, our souls could be physical when they needed to be, but I wasn't about to go too in-depth with that now. I didn't know why we lost some of our senses. We simply didn't need them anymore.

The Clock turned orange, which surprised me. The spirit before me never once asked about her death. She never recounted anything that happened in her life, like most souls did. She was here, and that was that. I had a feeling she knew there was no going back, so why bother? She thought this room was her bedroom, after all, and tried making the most of it.

It seemed all she needed was clarification about why she was still here, even though she was dead. Many people believe in going to some far-off paradise or be reincarnated. Once they had an understanding that the Spirit World is where everyone gathered and they had the free will to do whatever and go wherever they pleased, they were satisfied.

"What does that mean?" she pointed to The Clock.

"The session is almost over," I stated.

She nodded, standing. "I'm not upset I'm here, you know."

I grinned as The Clock turned red. I never thought she was.

"But if this is a place where you talk to new spirits, maybe liven the place up a bit?" she suggested. "Just a thought."

I watched her leave. When her spirit faded into the shadows, I whisked away her mug and mine. Then I waved my hand over the center of the table, causing a thin translucent vase to appear. It held a single blue rose.

I couldn't smell it, but it was pretty to look at.

***

"I still don't understand."

I suppressed a sigh. If I've had this conversation once, I've had it a thousand times. The spirit who sat before me convinced himself he was in heaven or hell. In the Living World, he was raised to believe in both. Now that he was in a black void—black being associated with all things bad, of course—he didn't know what to think.

"Where am I again?" he questioned.

"The Spirit World, or the Afterlife, as some call it," I stated.

"So, is it hell?"

"No."

"This can't be heaven."

"You're correct."

He groaned. "The Afterlife should be heaven or hell."

"But it's not. This is it," I said plainly.

"This can't be it."

"It is."

He sighed, taking a sip of his tea. When he arrived in the Crossover Room, he told me he didn't like tea when he was alive, but it was comforting to him now. I had already refilled his cup once. The spirit took slow sips, attempting to pace himself. However, it seemed his anxiety got the better of him. He tried doing anything to make himself feel better, but his knee bobbed up and down under the table.

"When the souls are alive," I began, "they attempt to learn about their surroundings and the way the world works. They learn about other people, how they got there, and what came to be. The Living World has a knack for trying to figure out the meaning of life, but it's a vast game of telephone."

He opened his mouth to respond, but I held up a hand to silence him so I could continue.

"What many alive souls believe in comes from books and stories passed down from generations. One person claims something—they heard something or saw something—and people believe it. But other than the written word, there's no actual proof it ever existed. People believe it and the story is told and retold for many years to come. Over time, it gets skewed and mistranslated. The story warps and people believe in different versions. Are you following me so far?"

He nodded along, sipping his tea. The soul never once took his eyes off me, genuinely interested in my words.

"You were raised to believe one thing, but depending on who you ask, your versions may or may not be correct."

"But it is correct," he said bluntly.

"Again, it depends on what they believe in," I stated. "No one knows the truth until they see it for themselves."

"How do I see the truth?" he questioned, leaning forward in his chair as though I was about to tell him the secret meaning of life.

"Well, you know it now. This is the Afterlife. You're a spirit."

"I'm dead?" he gasped.

I sighed.

"But wait, I'm just here? In this space?" he asked, waving his arms and gesturing around the room.

I nodded. "You can go back to the Living World as a spirit whenever you want, though. You can help those who are still alive. Or you can hang around here and be with the other souls."

"I can be alive again?"

"No, you can go back as a spirit."

He slouched in his chair, deep in thought. He peered into his mug, looked at me, holding it in my direction. I refilled the tea, and he blew on the steam.

After he drank some, he stared in my direction again. "So, if this isn't heaven or hell, then what is it?"

"It's the real Afterlife," I explained.

"But are we up or down? Above the clouds or below the surface?"

How could I explain this to him without causing him to think he was in one place over the other?

"We're on the same plane as the Living World," I explained, "but in our own area."

"That doesn't make sense," he replied bluntly.

"It does."

"I don't think so."

"You'll get used to it."

The room fell silent. We stared at one another for a few moments. Finally, he released a light chuckle. The spirit leaned forward, poking at the blue rose in the center of the table. His index finger went through the petals as though one of them were not real.

He stared at his finger like it was broken. "Did you kill me?" he questioned, not in a malicious tone, but with a confused one.

"I did not." I remained calm. "That's a rumor the Living World made up. I am not death, I'm the Grim Reaper. I have no control over who lives or who dies and when. I'm here to guide you to the Spirit World, help you understand your situation, and find peace in the Afterlife."

"That's nice of you."

"Thanks."

"But if you're not death, then who is?"

I was about to reply when I realized I wasn't sure of that answer. I couldn't say who or what death was. I turned my attention to The Clock, that still shone green.

"That's death?" the soul questioned in disbelief. He followed my gaze, pointed to the green circle staring us down on the other side of the room.

I had to think about it for a moment. "Well, everyone has an internal clock that looks like that one. From the moment a person is born, the clock ticks down. There are no numbers. It ticks in rhythm to the person's heart. The living counts up when a birthday passes, but the clock inside them ticks down, counting how much time they have left."

"How long do we have?" he asked.

I shrugged. "No one knows, and it's different for everyone. Everyone gets handed a different deck of cards, so to speak."

"So, freak accidents...?"

"Aren't so freaky."

"They're supposed to happen?"

"Yes," I nodded. "Expected and unexpected deaths are the same. Everyone leaves their physical form and arrives at the Spirit World when they're supposed to."

The spirit whistled. He pointed to the clock again. "So, then The Clock is death."

"If you want to believe The Clock is a sentient being, then sure."

"Who created The Clock?"

"No one. It's in all of us."

"Like an organ?"

"Sure," I replied. Although I didn't have an answer to that, either. "You know, some questions aren't meant to be answered. There'd be nothing left to learn otherwise."

He laughed, holding up his drink. "No, that means we wouldn't have to waste time in school. We'd live our lives so much earlier."

"Learning isn't limited to education," I stated.

He narrowed his eyes, tilting his head in confusion. The spirit nodded his head, gesturing for me to explain.

"In the beginning, sure. You learn about math, science, history, language... but there's more to life than academics. There are social skills, emotional responsibility, physical care, mental management, and so much more. Learning isn't limited to listening to a lecture or reading books about what others try to teach you.

"The best learning is through experiences, both alone and with others you care about. Learning is about making memories, overcoming tribulations, stepping out of your comfort zone, seeing what the world offers. If you know the answer to every question in existence, then there would be no living. There'd be nothing left to experience."

During my speech, the soul leaned forward on the table, resting his chin in his hands. He gazed at me, drinking in every word. Maybe he was finally beginning to understand.

In most sessions, I have to help the spirit understand their death and where to go from here. This guy, though, he was so confused with the Afterlife and why it was so different from what he was raised to believe. He comprehended life and death without knowing the true meaning of it all, not that he was supposed to know the meaning during his time in the Living World. Still, it was enough of an answer for him to continue living, even though he was dead. It allowed him to appreciate life and death as one.

He broke the silence, sitting up once more. "I think I finally get what people meant when they say to live your life to the fullest. We never know when our time is ending and we shouldn't take that for granted. I did my best not to, but it wasn't always easy."

"It's not supposed to be easy," I replied. "If it were easy—"

"There'd be no point in living," he finished my sentence with a grin.

I too smiled.

Shifting his weight in his chair, he leaned forward again, pushing his mug away. "I have another question, if you don't mind."

"Sure."

"How did you become the Grim Reaper?"

Left speechless, I hesitated to reply.

"I mean, how did you die and get this position?" he clarified.

I opened my mouth to respond with something—anything—but no words came out.

"Nah, I get it," the soul said, snickering. He flicked his wrist dismissively. "It's one of those questions I don't need to know the answer to, right?"

A nervous chortle escaped my lips, and all I could do was nod in agreement.

Being the Grim Reaper wasn't a job position. It simply was who I am. I'd been doing this for as long as I can remember. Now that I think about it, though, I don't remember ever being in the Living World.

How did I not know where I came from?

The Clock turned red, jolting me out of my thoughts. I hadn't noticed The Clock ever turning orange.

We said our goodbyes; the soul satisfied with our session. He felt better, understanding more about the Afterlife and what he could do now. The initial shock of it all had passed and now he planned on exploring the area more.

He left me to my own thoughts. It was always great to have a successful session with a spirit, helping them understand why they're here. How they arrived.

But how did I get here?

***

I sipped my coffee, listening to the soul sitting across the table from me discuss the many things he had done when he was alive. I didn't have favorites, but these sessions were always refreshing for me.

These spirits were already at peace with their death. Even though they didn't fully grasp where they were or why, they understood their death. Whatever they believed in when they were alive didn't matter anymore. They had the answers and accepted it.

This wasn't to say these spirits didn't miss being alive. No one is ever truly ready to die. However, that was why it was comforting for them to talk about the things they did and accomplished in the Living World.

It was comforting for me to hear, as well.

"I wrote a book when I was a teenager," the man continued his life's story after taking a sip of his beverage. "I wanted to publish it, but everyone told me I was too young. So, the book remained in my nightstand drawer; the bottom one, the junk drawer. I completely forgot about it. I didn't find it again until years later.

"In fact, I forgot about writing all together. I finished high school, completed college, and got a full-time job that had nothing to do with my degree. But I enjoyed my job all the same. It was what I really wanted to do," he chuckled. "People told me I wasted my talents because I had gotten a degree in something else. They told me I spent all my money on that piece of paper for nothing. But it wasn't a waste at all. I had so much knowledge in my brain! Just because I didn't actively use it in everyday life didn't mean I wasn't allowed to know it, you know?"

I nodded along, listening deeply to the man's words. "I agree. I've met many souls who believe they wasted so much time with schooling or any form of education because they didn't use the knowledge. But it's always good to have that wisdom in your back pocket."

"Exactly!" the man exclaimed. "I never viewed learning as a waste of time. Sure, it got expensive in the end, but how cool is it to join a discussion with others about something they assume you know nothing about? That's the only acceptable time to brag."

"Brag about teachings?"

"Brag about what you know, not what you've accomplished," he explained, tapping his temple with his index finger. "Everyone has accomplishments. Many accomplishments. Some big, some small, but we've all been there in different ways. But to know something someone else doesn't and have the ability to teach them something new? That's worth bragging about."

I grinned, remaining silent. I didn't want to interrupt.

"When I retired, guess what I found?" he continued. "That book I had written. I read it and, boy, was it awful! I'm glad I never published it. Quite embarrassing. Then again, it wasn't half bad for a 15-year-old's work.

"Anyway, that book inspired me to try writing again. I forgot what a love I had for it. I rewrote that story, a few others, and published them. I self-published them with the help of my grandchildren. Technology is a wonderful thing, but it was quite the learning curve for me," he explained, diverting from the topic.

I snickered at his words. I had seen technology grow and evolve in the Living World. I understand how important it was, but thankfully it hadn't made its way into the Spirit World. What a mess of things that would make.

"I self-published a few books, but they didn't do well. That's alright though," the soul continued speaking after another sip of his drink. "I did it for fun. My latest book, however, did well. Do you want to know what it was about?"

"What?" I played along.

"573 Things You Didn't Know You Needed to Know. I admit, the title could have used reworking. But people ate it up. Do you see what I mean about knowledge? People love learning whether they realize it or not."

"I agree. Many people don't realize you need to learn many subjects before you find the one you're truly interested in," I added.

"Yes, and when they find their niche, they crave knowledge," he agreed. "The book I wrote covered a wide range of topics, including life skills. I taught people how to change a flat tire, fix a leaky faucet... at least, according to people who reviewed my book. They boasted about how they learned things—useful things—they didn't learn from school or from their parents. I could teach them. I did that. I made a difference." He beamed, though the smile soon faded.

"Something wrong?" I prompted.

"I wrote another book," he said somberly.

"Did you?"

"I never finished it. I died."

"I see."

His smile returned. "It's alright. I know why I died."

"Why?" I questioned.

Although I knew how he had died. He was 92-years-old and his body crumbled from under him. His mind remained sharp as a tack, but his physical form couldn't handle it anymore. He fell asleep one night and didn't wake the next morning.

"I fulfilled my purpose in life," he said confidently.

"Purpose?"

"I helped others. People learned from me. I made a positive difference in their lives. I could share my knowledge," he explained.

I smiled affectionately at the old man.

"But they taught me something too," he continued. "I learned people are willing to learn as long as you make it accessible for them. Unfortunately, not everyone is so lucky." He stood, finishing the rest of his drink. "I can't wait to see what this next chapter brings me." He gazed around the empty space.

The Clock turned red and, for a moment, I felt as though the spirit dismissed himself rather than The Clock ending the session. I wasn't sure if that was possible, but it was clear this spirit knew what he was doing.

He was at peace and felt confident he fulfilled his purpose in life.

***

My gaze scanned the three souls sitting, drinks in front of them, all staring back at me. Introductions for these group sessions never got easier. It was one of the few times I didn't know what to say. Often these groups came together because one-on-one sessions didn't quite accomplish what I hoped. Or the spirits were alright, but needed a little extra help to mingle with the others. These group sessions were a great way to introduce them to one another.

I sat down in my chair, opening the discussion. "Anyone can begin the conversation. No rush."

The room fell silent. Two of the three spirits cast stares at each other, neither of them uttering a word. The elderly man sipped his tea, his lip curled upward into a smirk. I didn't expect much from him just yet. I invited him because I knew he'd be able to teach the other two.

As I was about to break the silence, the young woman pointed to the blue rose in the middle of the table.

"I see you've decorated," she said, winking at me.

I chuckled. "I did. Do you like it?"

"It looks great."

"Wait," the young man interjected, sitting forward. "There's a store here?"

"No," I replied, shaking my head.

He deflated back into his chair.

"Did you need something?" the woman questioned him.

He shrugged, staring at the ground. "Just thought if this place had a store, then that'd mean I'm in heaven."

The woman turned to me, brows furrowed in confusion. "I thought you said there wasn't such a thing as a good place or bad?"

"There isn't," I clarified. "What you were brought up to believe is speculation. In reality, there is no up or down, good or bad place, heaven or hell. There is only the Living World for those in their physical forms, alive, and the Spirit World, or Afterlife, for those whose souls have moved on from their physical forms. It doesn't matter what you did or didn't do in the Living World. Everyone arrives here when they die."

The young man stiffened, holding his hands up. "Wait, so are you saying there are... murderers here?"

"Yes," I responded honestly. I've met them all.

He shuddered, recoiling back into his chair again.

The woman laughed. "That's pretty cool, actually. I wish we could have our own bedrooms, though. I'd love to see how a murderer decorates."

"I don't want to meet a murderer," the man stated. He turned his head to look at her, twisting his face with disgust at her suggestion.

"Why not?" she asked.

"I don't want to get on their bad side."

"They can't do anything to you now. We're all dead."

He shuddered again as I sighed. This conversation certainly turn an odd turn.

"May I say something?" the old man piped up.

"Yes, please," I invited.

The older gentleman looked at the younger spirit with kind eyes. "I don't believe we need to be afraid of any soul who is here with us. Whatever they did or didn't do in their previous life doesn't reflect on who they are as a spirit."

The young man arched a brow. "You mean, when they died, they suddenly learned their lessons?"

"It depends on what lesson you mean."

"Good from bad?"

"What defines being good? And how would you define bad?"

"Killing people is bad," the woman said, joining the conversation with a raised hand.

The old man nodded his head to her. "Yes, I'm not arguing that, but how do you suppose they got to that point in their life?"

She shook her head, bringing her hand back to her lap. "There's no way to know unless we get to know them."

"Exactly."

The young man slouched in his chair, crossing his arms over his chest. "I still don't think I want to get to know a murderer."

"Everyone is born with innocence," I added. "Those souls who did unspeakable things when they were alive did so because of the path they walked. That doesn't mean it's right, but, unfortunately, some lives are lived that way."

"So, we're lucky because we didn't walk down a dark path that caused us to kill people?" our interior decorator friend inquired.

"In a way, yes," the elderly man agreed with me, "but it's also about perspective. What you consider good or bad is not considered so to someone else."

"I think killing another is universally bad," the young gentleman stated defiantly.

The old man chuckled. "Let's forget about killing for a moment. That's a harsh example. Think about anything you'd consider bad. Anything at all, it doesn't have to be as extreme as murder, but it also doesn't have to be as small as driving past a pedestrian on the crosswalk."

The woman snorted a laugh. "I used to do that all the time."

"See?" the gentleman pointed to her while looking at the younger man. "Would you consider her bad?"

"No," he replied indifferently. "I used to do that sometimes, too. But it doesn't mean she did it on purpose. Sometimes you did it because you're in a rush, but also sometimes you don't see them on the side of the road until the last minute and you're going too fast to stop."

"True," the woman responded, "but I'll say I did it on purpose a lot." She chuckled in my direction. "I liked to drive fast."

I pressed my lips into a smirk. I didn't know whether to laugh along or stare in disbelief. The gentleman facilitated this conversation quite nice. So, I brought my mug to my lips, drinking, and letting the conversation continue as is.

The old man leaned closer to the young man. "What if someone stole something from the store? Would you consider that bad?"

"Yes, of course," he replied.

"But you don't know why they stole. You didn't even question what they stole."

"Doesn't matter. Stealing is bad."

"But what if it was from the grocery store?"

The young man hesitated for a moment before shaking his head. "It's still bad. You can't steal from others, even from a corporation, no matter how bad you need it. There are other ways to get help. They can ask family or friends."

"But what if they're on their own?" the woman chimed in.

He shook his head. "Again, there are other ways to get food."

"What if they're too proud or embarrassed?" the gentleman pressed.

"That's something they need to get over themselves if they want to survive," the young man said curtly.

The woman whistled. "Wow... so, you're saying that you'd excuse no one if they did something you didn't agree with?"

The young man paused for a moment. "Well, no. I wouldn't say that. Who am I to judge what's right and what's wrong?"

The room fell silent. The woman pressed her lips together, holding back a smirk, while the gentleman bowed his head knowingly. I, too, stared at him in shock.

Then the young man pinched the bridge of his nose. "Alright, fine. You got me."

"May I ask one more question?" the old man asked.

The young gentleman sighed. "Go for it."

"What would you do if you saw someone stealing from the grocery store?"

"Probably nothing. It's not my problem."

"Then you'd be part of the problem by letting the person get away with stealing," the woman stated.

He reached forward, grabbing his drink. As he took a long sip, it became obvious he now avoided continuing the conversation.

"I think we've unpacked a lot here," I interjected, ending the debate. "I think we can all agree that we shouldn't judge someone based on their actions, from what they did or didn't do. Especially from when they were alive. Because, now, you're all one with your soul, and what you did in your physical form no longer matters. It's up to you on how you want to deal with your own actions going forward."

"Do any of the murderers here regret what they did?" The woman questioned.

I nodded. "Some feel remorse, others don't. Some did it on purpose and others didn't. Every spirit's story is unique from the previous one."

I turned my attention to the young man still chugging his drink. Although, I was sure his cup was empty by now. "I'm sure you did things in your physical form you don't agree with now. But there are many other things you did that you'd boast about. I guarantee if you told us all your experiences, we wouldn't share the same emotions as you with each story. We're all born innocent. However, the people we meet, the events that occur in our lives, and the choices we make all influence our life's path. Sometimes you're steering and sometimes you're not."

The woman raised her hand again. I nodded, signaling she could speak. "Basically, despite what we did when we were alive, we all have a clean slate here?"

"Yes," I agreed.

"But we also remember our previous lives. So, we need to carry those burdens with us, whether we agree with our actions or not," the young man added.

The elderly gentleman piped up. "Yes, but there's no need to judge ourselves or others in the Spirit World. They were judged enough in the Living World, I'm sure. What the spirits need now, what we all need, is peace and acceptance."

The young man straightened in his seat. He smiled for the first time. "So, this isn't heaven or hell because, in the Afterlife, we're all equal."

I nodded, smiling at his realization.

While this group session did not go as I originally thought, the conversation turned out well. The spirits seemed to each learn something and understand the Afterlife further. The three dismissed themselves as The Clock turned red, leaving me alone with my thoughts.

The truth was, all souls were equal in the Afterlife because they were already equal in the Living World. Humans had a habit of putting themselves and certain groups on pedestals. The notion that supposed good people would have it made in the Afterlife and so-called bad people would be damned for all eternity was utterly ridiculous.

But I wasn't here to help the living live. I was here to help the dead live.

THE FIFTH GROUP

THE WOMAN SITTING ACROSS the table from me sipped her coffee casually. She barely cast a glance in my direction. "I didn't come to you because I don't know what my peace is."

I nodded along, though her eyes were closed with her coffee mug pressed against her lips. "I'm happy to hear you've found your peace."

"But I think I'm broken," she said.

"Broken?"

"My soul. It's broken. Or maybe it's my brain... do I have a brain?"

Technically, no. She didn't have a brain anymore. Brains were an organ that fit within the skeletal host, protected by the outer skin layer of the physical forms inhabiting the Living World. Now her soul did the work of her brain, carrying memories and feelings from her time alive.

"My point," she continued before I could reply, "is I don't know the truth."

I thought about her words for a moment, hoping I understood. "It sounds like you haven't found your peace, then?"

"No, I did," she breathed out a sigh of annoyance. I let her continue, unsure if that irritated response geared toward me or the situation.

She spoke in a calmer tone now. "I'm fine that I'm dead. I didn't have a glorious life to begin with, but it was fun while it lasted. Good and bad things happened. That's the way it goes. I didn't make a significant impact on the world, but I had many good times."

"Then it sounds like you have found your peace, if you're truly happy with your life," I responded. Although I knew there was more to it. To keep her irritation at bay, I went along with whatever she said. If she thought she found her peace, then there was a chance she had already. Who was I to say otherwise? Still, something didn't sit right.

"I want to know the truth," she said.

"What truth?" I genuinely didn't know what she had in mind.

She drew in a sharp breath, leaning forward. She looked me in the eye, putting down her mug. "I want to know everything that's happened when I wasn't around."

I narrowed my eyes in confusion. "You mean after you crossed over into the Spirit World?"

"No, when I was alive."

I didn't answer, totally lost to what she wanted. Thankfully, I didn't need to egg her on for clarification.

"I had a couple of boyfriends in my lifetime and one of them cheated on me. I figured it out eventually, but I want to know when it started. I never found out the whole truth. I want to know what people said about me behind my back. When my mother died, I wasn't in the room. I was late. I want to know what I missed. I want to know it all."

I relaxed into my chair, finally understanding what she wanted—what she thought she needed. It wasn't uncommon for a soul to cross over with the assumption they'd suddenly discover all of life's secrets. I didn't understand why they thought that. What would the souls do with this information once they had it? Maybe those who believed in reincarnation thought they'd take those memories and teachings with them into their next life.

Unfortunately, that's not how things worked around here.

She frowned at the heavy silence. "I am broken, aren't I?"

"No, not at all. You're not the only one to think you'd know everything about crossing over," I reassured her.

"But I'm the only one who didn't get that information?"

"No, you're not. No one knows."

"But then...?"

I held up a hand to silence her. "Let me ask you why you didn't already have these answers when you were alive."

"I wasn't there when it happened. I'd get bits and pieces of information from others, but could never complete the puzzle," she explained.

"Right, because there are three sides to every story," I said.

"Excuse me?"

"This person's side, that person's side, and the truth. No one ever knows what the truth is because everyone's truth is skewed to benefit themselves."

She cast her gaze away, deep in thought. "You're saying my friends lied to me?"

"No," I said, shaking my head. "Your friends told you what they thought was right. Or, they shared with you what they saw. Perception is everything. Eyes play tricks and so do the ears. Whatever people hear or see gets blown out of proportion to protect themselves or someone they love. Thus, the truth gets skewed. So, no. Your friends didn't lie to you. Not on purpose, anyway."

The woman's gaze wandered the empty room. She nodded along with my words and I could see the cogs turning as she thought about what I said.

"Have you ever played a game of telephone?" I asked.

She nodded.

"And how often did the exact phrase get from one person to the last in line?"

She chuckled. "Never." Then she paused. "Oh, I see what you're saying! But how can I learn the truth now?"

I shrugged. "You can't."

"But I thought I'd be able to go back to the Living World and wander as a spirit?"

"That you can do."

"So, I can spy on people?"

"In the present."

Her brows furrowed.

"Everything that happened occurred in the past," I explained. "You can't go back in time. You can only go from the Spirit World to the Living World and back again in real time. The present."

She deflated, melting into her chair. "So, I'll never know the truth?" she asked quietly.

"You know *your* truth," I corrected. "Despite all that, did you learn from the things that happened?"

"Yeah," she said, sitting up again. "Actually, it was because of that boyfriend who cheated on me I found my husband. I vented to a random customer at work and we hit things off."

"Would you change that?"

"No, of course not."

"What do you think would have happened if you knew the situation any differently?" I questioned.

She paused. Her expression relaxed, and I could see something resonated with her.

"You're right," she said, grinning. "Everything happened as it was supposed to. If I knew something different about my cheating ex, then I might have tried to get him to stay with me. Or I might have called out of work that day and never met my husband. Everything happens for a reason."

The Clock turned red, and we said our goodbyes. The soul left with a wide grin on her face and a spring in her step.

I watched her exit, knowing things didn't always happen for a reason. Fate knew how long a soul would last in the Living World, but it didn't have each life mapped out from start to finish. It was another misconception the Living World made up.

But, for now, I'd let this spirit have her truth.

***

"Coffee? Tea?" I offered.

The soul stared blankly ahead, shrugging her shoulders. She sat slouched in her chair, hugging herself as tight as her vapor self could.

"Do you like chocolate?" I pressed gently.

She barely moved her head, but I caught the nod. I flicked my wrist and a mug of steaming hot cocoa appeared in front of her and me. I picked up my drink, taking a sip. Almost all the souls I met prefer coffee or tea, but hot chocolate was a good option once in a while.

The woman hesitated, but she picked up her mug, sipping it. I detected a small grin hiding behind the steam, but she still didn't look at me.

"Feeling better?" I asked.

Her shoulders relaxed as she drew in the scent of her beverage. She exhaled through her mouth contently.

"I used to make hot chocolate all the time. It was something I'd do for the kids at family parties and stuff. I had a lot of younger cousins, but no siblings of my own," she explained.

"It's such a simple drink, yet comforting. It's not just good for snowy days, either. It's also good for sad days. Tough days. Days when you need to catch up with an old friend."

I nodded in agreement, though she continued speaking.

"The kids used to love making hot cocoa with me. I never bought the packets. My mother used to make it from scratch when I was a kid, so that's what I did." She finally looked in my direction, grinning excitedly. "Then I'd set up a little buffet. I'd add chocolate spoons, peppermint sticks, or cinnamon sticks for stirrers. I'd also have mini marshmallows, cinnamon sugar, whipped cream, mini chocolate chips, sometimes caramel sauce to drizzle on the whipped cream..." she hummed, closing her eyes, lost in a memory.

"That sounds lovely," I answered encouragingly. If I were being honest, I'd say I was jealous. Her story made me wish I could create elaborate drink bars for the souls here. But none of us could enjoy it thoroughly.

She placed her cup down on the table, releasing a somber sigh. "What's going to happen to them now that I'm gone?"

I arched a brow at her awareness. She wasn't concerned about her life and why she was here like so many other souls. This spirit was more concerned about the people she left behind in the Living World.

"They'll continue their lives," I said simply. "It won't be the same for them without you being there, of course, but life goes on."

She peeled her gaze away from me, leaning back in her chair. She stared out into the void. I knew she didn't want to hear that answer, but it was the only one I could give.

"They'll be alright," I continued reassuringly. "It'll take time, but they'll carry on your legacy. They'll remember and cherish the memories you made with them. What did you guys do when you had hot chocolate together?" I requested her to share more memories with me, to talk it through some more.

The small smile returned to her lips. She brought the hot chocolate close to her chest. "We talked about our days. My cousins would discuss school. Relationship drama. Complain about homework. The older ones talked about work—they're co-workers, customers... we talked about anything and everything. We didn't see each other too often, so when we did, we caught up and got to know each other."

"It sounds like you made many memories with them," I stated.

"Many moments make memories," she said. "It was just hot chocolate but, I think, it was the highlight for many of us. It was for me, anyway. But... now that's all over."

I shook my head. "I don't think so. I believe someone will keep up the tradition you started."

"Tradition?"

"It was something you always did at family gatherings, and it was something yourself and your cousins always looked forward to. I'd call that a tradition."

The woman cracked a small smile, though I knew that was an attempt at being polite. "I guess you could call it tradition. But I won't be there anymore. It'll be great if they continue it, but I'll miss a lot."

"You won't miss anything you don't want to," I explained. "You can go back to the Living World and watch over your loved ones."

"I can?" she sat taller in her seat.

I nodded. It was strange how many souls didn't know they could wander between the Living World and Spirit World. When alive, they thought their loved ones watched over them. It was a comforting thought. But, when arriving in the Afterlife, they seemed to forget that. Out of all the ridiculous rumors they believed in when alive, did they not actually believe the souls of past loved ones were with them?

"I can still share hot chocolate with them? I can listen in on their conversations?" she questioned.

"Yes, though you won't be able to speak to them. You also won't be able to drink the hot chocolate." I hadn't realized a beverage of all things would get this soul talking and feel more comfortable. Scents and sounds often triggered memories, so it made sense. Maybe I needed to expand my menu for them.

"I understand," she replied quietly, "but I can still be present. It'll be tough at first not being able to add to the conversation, but I'm not ready to let them go just yet."

"Many souls aren't ready to let go of their lives upon arriving here. That's normal," I said reassuringly.

She laughed. "My life was one bad luck streak after another. I'm good being here."

My mouth gaped open in shock.

"I almost joined you a few years ago, but I didn't. I dropped out of high school, and tried college for a little while, but it wasn't for me. I got decent jobs, though. However, I had a hard time sticking with them. The economy went down the tubes once or twice. I got laid off or the company would close. There were so many times I wasn't needed anymore. But you know where I was always needed?" she asked, holding up her mug.

"My cousins. My family. It wasn't much, but it was something everyone looked forward to. People appreciated the time and effort I put into making a hot chocolate bar to set aside time to spend with them." She chuckled. "It sounds like such a small thing, doesn't it? Making hot chocolate isn't such a revelation."

"You don't need to make a difference for everyone. Even just making a difference for one person is enough," I stated.

She nodded along. "It's true. So, I don't know why my time in the Living World got cut so short. I'll never know why fate would have me get hit by a bus. There's still so much I could have done... but I guess I'll hold on to the memories. Nothing can take those away."

The Clock turned red. Despite her wanting to do more, to continue being there for her family, she seemed satisfied with the outcome. Knowing she could go back to the Living World was all the reassurance she needed.

Sometimes it was better that way. I wasn't allowed to skew the memories a soul brought with them, and I certainly wasn't allowed to correct them when they recounted their death wrong. Some deaths were too traumatic for the spirit. She remained unaware that she hit the bus. It was parked, and she collided with it when she looked down at her phone while driving.

However, if it made her feel better believing the bus hit her, then I'd let her believe it as long as it helped her hold on to those moments.

***

I've seen spirits go through all the stages of grief. Some of those conversations were easier than others. Sometimes the spirit talked to themselves about their feelings and I was merely a sound board. Other times, I spoke to the spirit with everything I had, trying to help them understand and feel better. The soul sitting across the table from me now was a mixed bag of emotions.

I had given her a cup of tea, as requested. She didn't drink from it, only breathed in its scent from time to time. Surely, it was cold by now, but when I asked if she wanted a refill, she ignored me.

Well, I don't think she was ignoring me. She simply looked out the sightless window, lost in her own thoughts. It was almost as though she saw something out the window, but I couldn't read her mind. I didn't know what she reminisced about.

At one point, I noticed a tear roll down her cheek. However, she quickly wiped it away, as though embarrassed. Then another tear appeared on the same cheek and she didn't seem to notice.

"Is there something you'd like to talk about?" I coaxed gently.

No response.

I leaned back in my chair, trying to seem casual. "I can answer any question you have. If you're willing, I'm here to help guide you through your thoughts."

She didn't answer, but I noticed her gaze glance in my direction for a moment. When she saw I looked back at her, she pivoted away and focused outside the window again.

"Are you afraid of me?" I wondered aloud. It wasn't uncommon for the spirits to fear my presence. My name had a fair amount of gossip surrounding it. I prepared myself to explain yet again that I was here to help. I didn't kill anyone and bring them here against their will. I explained it time and time again.

However, that one question got the soul's attention, and she finally looked me in the eye.

"Afraid of you?" she repeated, her tone suggested offense at my words. "Why would I be afraid of you, of all things?"

Now it was my turn to remain silent. Not many spirits rendered me speechless, but this took a turn I didn't expect.

"Out of everything I've been through," she turned her full body to face me now, "why would I be afraid of *you?*"

Spirits were afraid of me for many reasons, though I wasn't about to get into it. I chose not to respond as I saw fire dancing in her gaze.

As predicted, she continued speaking. "I've witnessed many scary moments in my life. This doesn't come close to what I've been through. At least I know I can finally relax here." She turned her gaze to her teacup. Instead of sipping it, she drew in its scent again. Chamomile. I often chose that to keep a spirit comfortable.

After a deep breath, she spoke again. "The scariest moment of my life was when I knew I was going to die. Not because I didn't know what was to come next. Not because I didn't know what would happen to my soul in the beyond. But because of my children. My grandchildren," she explained, frowning.

"I believe I raised my children well. We had a decent relationship. When they grew older, moved out of the house, and started their own families, I was always there for them. I helped them with questions about moving house. Questions about pregnancy. About raising children. Financial matters. I did everything for my kids and while I knew they were grateful, I was terrified."

I watched in silence as she glared into her teacup, gripping it tighter. She fought back more tears, visibly shaking.

"What if I steered them in the wrong direction?" she asked through gritted teeth. "What if I gave them the wrong answers? Their generation is so different from how I grew up. The information I gave them must be outdated. Do you understand how worrying that is for a mother?" She snapped her attention away from the tea, looking at me, eyes wide with horror. "One wrong move and I've screwed up my children's entire future."

Suddenly feeling a warm comfort for this woman, I pressed my lips into a sad smile. She wasn't stressed about being here. She stressed her children weren't ready to lose their mother, about steering them in the wrong direction before leaving them behind.

"We can never do enough for our children," I stated.

She perked up before I could continue. "Do you have children?"

"No."

The woman frowned again.

"My point," I continued, "is that as a parent, you do what you believe is right for your children. You raise them to ensure they make their own decisions that are right for them. Your worry proves to me you were an excellent mother. You don't have to be afraid of whether you gave them the right or wrong information. They'll figure things out for themselves in due time with your advice in their back pocket."

She nodded along, turning her gaze downward.

"You can also go back to the Living World whenever you want. You can still help them, though it'll look different."

"No," she said softly. "Maybe someday, but I can't right now."

I shut my mouth, hoping she'd elaborate.

"When I was sick, knowing I'd die soon, my children took turns visiting me," she began. "The hospital only allowed a certain number of people in the room at once. I had four children, and they were all married with children of their own. They'd come in shifts, often not giving me much of a break. I didn't get much peace or alone time. They assumed I didn't want to be alone during my last nights, but I also didn't want them to see me the way I was.

"It was hard enough for my children to see me in that state, but my grandchildren? I understand they wanted to say goodbye. I'm not saying I wasn't grateful I got to see them one last time, but a hospital is no place for children. They shouldn't have had to see their grandmother like that," she said, her voice cracking.

She drew in a sharp breath. "My kids were somber, upset about my situation. It was heartbreaking being surrounded by such pity. My grandchildren openly wept. Do you know what I did?"

"What did you do?" I requested gently.

"I smiled," she said, forcing a grin. She sat taller in her chair for a moment before relaxing her shoulders once more. The spirit tried keeping the smile, but it transitioned into a frown again. "I told them I was ready. That I couldn't wait to see my husband again. I lived a good life, and I was ready to see what was on the other side. It made them happy. They'd smile back at me and say how excited they were for me. They said they hoped they were just as ready as I was when they get to that point in their life."

Her shoulders shook. "But the truth is... I lied. I wasn't ready. I was terrified. I didn't know what would happen next. I didn't know if it'd be painful. No offense, but I wasn't looking forward to death being my next grand adventure. I didn't want to leave my family behind. But I did what I had to do. I put on a brave face. I smiled because that's what mothers do for their children." She choked back a few tears. "It's nothing for them to look up to. I'm a fraud."

I leaned forward, resting my arms on the table. "You're not a fraud," I said sternly. "There's nothing wrong with what you did. Everyone is afraid of the Afterlife. No one is ever ready to arrive here. Now that you are here, would you say it's that bad?"

She lifted her head, looking around, even though there wasn't anything to see. Eventually, her gaze landed on me. "No, actually. This isn't at all what I expected it to be, but I don't mind it. It's odd, but peaceful."

"I'm glad to hear that," I grinned. "I'm sure your family knows you're in a good place, even though it's not quite home. You did what you felt was right for your children at the moment. And that was to put on a brave face for them because you love them. Do you think your children saw through it?"

She tilted her head upward, thinking. "I'm not sure. One of my sons might have thought I was faking, but I couldn't say for certain. I know my grandchildren took it in stride. They were happy for me. My children were excited for me too, but maybe it was an act for their children."

"Would you say they put on a brave face for their kids?"

The woman stiffened, looking at me with shock. A sly grin appeared on her face. "Ah, I see what you're trying to do."

"I'm not trying to do anything," I replied casually. "You're worried you didn't always give the best advice or steered your children in the wrong direction, but it seems to me they learned a lot from you. No, a hospital isn't the best place for young children to be, but your kids wanted their kids to have one last moment with their grandmother. Death is part of life and they wanted their children to experience that moment. It opens up many intriguing and important conversations."

She nodded, a genuine smile forming on her lips. "I suppose you're right."

"You did what you believe any mother should do for her children and grandchildren, which makes it right. Your kids are doing the same for their kids. Maybe they could see through your brave smile. Maybe they knew you were scared and were also putting on a brave face for you."

I watched as her eyes filled up again, though the smile never left her face. It never occurred to her that her children put on brave faces for her sake.

"That was their way of letting you know you did your job and did it well. They love you and they'll be alright without you. They'll miss you, of course, but you have nothing to worry about."

With little hesitation, the spirit openly wept in front of me. Finally, she let out all her emotions. She laughed as she cried, tilting her head back and shouting into the void. She wiped streams of tears off her face, attempting to catch her breath.

Then The Clock turned red.

***

Another group session was in progress. I had three ladies seated around the table conversing over the hot chocolate I had given them all. Automatically, I gave one spirit cocoa, knowing it held fond memories for her. The other women requested it as well, now they knew it was an option. I watched the three discuss their beverages, as though they've never had hot chocolate before. They were all satisfied and content.

I listened in on their conversation, sipping my beverage. I didn't want to interrupt. They didn't know each other in the Living World, but they sure acted as though they did. The trio clicked so well together; they sat around the table, catching up like old friends.

"You'd let them add mini chocolate chips or syrup on top of the whipped cream?" the eldest questioned.

The youngest responded with a nod of her head. "The kids loved it."

"Isn't that a lot of sugar?" the third chimed in.

"Not at all. It's not like I gave it to the kids with every meal. It was a once in a while thing."

"Oh, I see."

"I find that to be too much chocolate. Too sweet for me. But it's certainly a nice gesture," the eldest added her two cents, sipping her drink.

"Thank you," the youngest replied.

"But you never had kids of your own?" the middle-aged woman inquired.

The adolescent of the three shook her head. "Nope. Never got married."

"I didn't have kids, either. I got married, but we couldn't have children. It was tough to hear at first."

"I'm sorry."

"It's alright. Life had other things in store for us."

"I'm sure you had many memories," the youngest replied.

"We did," the middle-aged woman responded with a grin. "We traveled a lot."

"I had children," the oldest piped up. "Lots of grandchildren, too. I spoiled them, but not in the way of this hot chocolate. I'm sorry I didn't think of it myself." She sipped her beverage, thoroughly enjoying its sweet warmth.

I chuckled into my drink. This was the first time I've had a group session where the three spirits forgot I was in the room. That was fine by me, though. These ladies were settling into the Afterlife, and their conversation pushed them along.

They had a few things in common. One, they all were disappointed by what they left behind, worried about the people from their previous lives. Two, they held onto deep memories from their previous lives. Arriving at the Afterlife was never an easy situation to cope with, especially when they felt they still had so much to live for.

"I'm sorry I'll never be able to do this ever again with the people I love. I can be there in spirit as they make hot chocolate, but it won't be the same."

"It was nice while it lasted, I'm sure. It's weird not being with my husband anymore, though. Still, I too can go back to the Living World and hang around him."

"And I wish I could have remained with my family, but honestly? Now that I'm finally here, I feel good knowing I can rest."

The other two giggled.

The eldest continued. "I had a stressful life, always making sure my family had what they needed. I wouldn't change a thing, mind you, but... I don't know. It feels kind of nice that I don't have to worry about it anymore. Is that rude of me to say?"

"Not at all," the middle-aged woman replied. "We're in the Afterlife. We're meant to rest and be at peace."

"It's never great losing a loved one," the youngest added, "but they'll always have the memories. They'll reminisce about the moments they shared with you and remember the words you shared with them. They'll cherish those lessons."

"You're right. Those moments are remembered forever, big or small," the eldest replied.

I noticed The Clock turned orange. Despite how out of place I felt, I was pleased they all got along so well.

"When I got here," the middle-aged lady began, "I harped on things that happened when I was alive that don't even matter. I happily married my husband because of something bad that happened to me. I was so desperate to find out the truth behind my cheating ex, but the truth doesn't matter. The truth is, the situation sucked at first, but I found happiness at the end of that dark tunnel."

I grinned, delighted she found her truth in the end.

The youngest nodded along. "My life wasn't shiny all the time, either. I had a rough go. But the people around me made it much better. I think that's why I was so fixated on hot chocolate. It's simple, but it was something I created and shared. I created a tradition for my family. How cool of a legacy is that?"

"It sounds like we all have that in common. We all found happiness through the hard times in life. We created memories and those moments are truth enough. They define who we are."

The ladies agreed with one another as The Clock turned red. They continued conversing as they exited the Crossover Room, leaving me behind. They thanked me for my time, but they certainly didn't need my help anymore.

Which made me wonder: what's my happiness? I enjoyed helping spirits move on, but those spirits didn't even need me in the room to figure things out for themselves. Yet, I was still here. I'd always be here.

What was my truth?

THE SIXTH GROUP

"Why did you bring me here?"

"You've passed on from the Living World into the Spirit World," I replied casually.

The spirit stood beside their chair on the other side of the table. His eyes scanned frantically around the room, desperate for an escape. He folded his arms across his chest defensively, body stiff, standing tall. I'm not sure, but I think he thought I was there to hurt him.

Nothing could hurt him, though. He was a spirit. That was the ironic part about being dead. When a person was alive, many things could hurt them physically and emotionally. They'd suffer at the hands of other people, mostly. It was rare they'd get hurt by something else, unless it was an illness or a natural disaster. But, in death, the only one who would hurt a spirit was themselves.

Spirits couldn't physically get hurt, but they could still feel emotionally wounded. Rarely was it the fault of other souls. It depended on how quick they found their peace.

"Why am I here?" he demanded again, glaring at me.

I pointed to the teacup on the table. "Would you like to sit down? Then we can chat."

He eyed the drink suspiciously before casting that gaze to me. However, he didn't respond as he sat down, slowly, as though trying not to make any sudden movements. The spirit never picked up his teacup.

"Would you care for a different beverage?" I asked.

"Tell me why I'm here," he commanded again.

"You're dead," I replied in a gentle tone, though it was on the cusp of annoyance.

"You killed me?"

"No, you died from other circumstances. I brought you here so you can be at peace."

"If you're not the one who killed me, then how did you know I died?"

I stared blankly back at him, unsure of how to answer. I was the Grim Reaper; I knew when everyone died. It was up to me to collect their souls from the Living World so they didn't wander too far, getting lost before arriving in the Spirit World. I didn't know how I came to that knowledge, though. I just knew.

"You killed me," he stated outright. "You're the Grim Reaper, right?"

I sighed, knowing where this was headed. "Yes, but—"

"Then you killed me!" he raised his voice, standing again. "You ripped me from my life. You stole my soul from my body!"

Stole his soul? That was certainly a new one.

I put my hands up in surrender. "Whatever you believe about the Grim Reaper isn't true. I do not kill people. I'm here to help you crossover from the Living World to the Afterlife safely."

"If this is the Afterlife, then why is it so dark?"

"I didn't create it."

"Then who did?"

"Fate."

To be honest, I wasn't sure. But this is how things worked in the Afterlife. I assumed fate had a hand in it.

The soul sneered at me, standing tall again. "You really expect me to believe you're not fate?"

"You told me I'm the Grim Reaper, so I believe you're aware I'm not fate," I replied simply.

"Fate is death, and death is the Grim Reaper."

"Fate is many things. Fate can be something happening that causes you not to get that new job you wanted, but something better arises from it. Something happens that helps steer you in a different direction."

"No," he shook his head. "You're talking about destiny."

"Fate and destiny are the same," I corrected.

"Destiny dictates the path you walk."

"You all walk on the same path."

"No, we take different turns. Everyone leads a different life."

"True," I agreed, "but—"

"Destiny pushes you toward your fate," he continued.

"But you said fate is death."

"Yes."

"So, what you're saying is that everyone's fate is to die?"

He opened his mouth to retaliate, but no words came out. Instead, the spirit shut his mouth, turning a confused gaze away, deep in thought.

I pointed to his seat again. "Please sit down so we can talk this through."

He scratched the top of his head as he sat. "Wait, so you *are* fate! If everyone's fate is to die, and you're the Grim Reaper, which is also death, then... wait."

"Can I please explain?" I asked calmly. To my surprise, he nodded.

"I am the Grim Reaper, yes, but death is separate. Death strikes when your internal clock runs out. Then, I arrive to help bring you to the Spirit World so you may find peace. Fate, or destiny, if you want to call it, is entirely different. It's part of the internal clock."

"What internal clock?" the spirit questioned.

I pointed to the large green faceless clock hanging in the room. "Every living physical form has that inside of them when they're born. The clock ticks down and when it reaches zero, you die. No one sees the internal clock. No one knows it's there inside them, but it's part of them. Everyone has a different amount of time given to them. I don't know what that time is or why. It's decided by fate. You died not because of me, but because your internal clock reached zero. Fate decided when your time was up, death claimed you, and then I came to pick you up."

The spirit didn't respond, though he watched me closely. He hugged himself again, tightening his posture. I sipped my coffee, ignoring the sour expression on his face. I said my piece, so I'd leave the ball in his court now.

His reaction and anger didn't bother me. I've dealt with with spirits before, blaming me for their death, thinking I had killed them. However, there was only so much I could do to convince them. They needed an open mind, but they didn't have any choices. They were dead. There was no going back.

As I put my coffee cup down on the table, I noticed the spirit gazing out the window. His expression turned from bitterness to sadness.

"Most people believe death is a bad thing," I breathed. "But it's not. It's simply part of life."

He slowly turned his head to face me, all hostility gone. "But dying means life ends."

I shook my head. "On the contrary. Death means a new beginning. What did you think would happen to you when you died?"

The soul tilted his chin upward, thinking. "I've never thought about it before. I thought it would be similar to before I existed. Nothingness. No senses, no memories. Empty."

"You thought you'd cease to exist?"

"I guess so, yeah."

I looked at our surroundings. Sure enough, the Afterlife was pretty empty. There was nothing to look at. A void surrounded us. In a weird way, he was kind of right about what this place would be like when he died.

"But now, let me ask you," I continued, "do you remember where you are?"

"You told me the Afterlife," he replied softly.

I nodded. "Say it again."

"Afterlife?" he said, confused.

"After life," I intoned slow. "Dying doesn't mean you stop living. You're simply starting a new beginning. A new life, so to speak."

The soul tilted his head to the side. "You mean to say life doesn't die with death?"

"You're here, aren't you?"

I picked up my coffee, and he followed my movements, drinking his tea. His face scrunched in disgust. He put the tea down, pushing the mug away from him.

"If life continues here, then what about my family? My friends? My job?" he questioned.

"Whoever has passed on is here somewhere. You'll be able to find them and reconnect. Otherwise, you can go back to the Living World and be with those you care about in spirit," I explained.

"They won't know I'm there?"

"Some might. It depends if they keep an open mind."

"But how am I supposed to go back to work?"

I chuckled. Most spirits were pleased they didn't have to go to work anymore. "No need to worry about work or finances. The only work that needs to be done here is finding your peace."

"How do I find peace?" he asked.

"I can't answer that for you. Everyone's peace is different."

"But how will I know when I find peace?"

"You'll just know."

He leaned back in his chair, unsatisfied. I understood how confusing it was. It frustrated me, too. However, the spirits needed to figure these things out for themselves. If I made suggestions, then the souls would assume that's what they're supposed to do.

So, we remained silent for a bit. I could see the cogs turning in his mind. Finally, he leaned forward, burying his face in the palms of his hands.

"I don't understand any of this," he groaned.

"I don't expect you to. It's a lot to process," I stated.

He dropped his hands onto the table, lifting his head to look at me. "What's my purpose here?"

I shook my head, and he rolled his eyes before I could reply.

"I need to figure it out for myself?" he asked. I nodded.

"So, I live to figure out my purpose in life and make money and pay bills, only to die and have to find my purpose here, too, while helping my family as a spirit?"

I hesitated for a moment. When he put it like that, it didn't sound appealing at all.

"There's more to it," I replied. "But it's something you'll discover soon enough."

He chuckled. "I thought dying would be a break from life, but it's still complicated."

"Life and death are complicated subjects," I said. "If we understood life, and we understood death, there would be no purpose to either."

"But we'd enjoy life. We'd find peace in death much faster," he countered.

"It's the journey, not the destination."

Most people took life for granted. As much as they wished for time to slow down, they often rushed. They prioritized too much of one thing over another, often regretting those priorities by the end. Living should be simple, but they make it complicated.

Death isn't complicated. There's no rush for spirits to find their peace or to decide what they want to do next. Peace was easy to come by as long as they kept an open mind and paid attention. I hoped this spirit, much like all the souls I've encountered, didn't take death for granted.

***

When the next spirit had entered the Crossover Room, she was quiet and hesitant. When she finally sat down at the table, she meekly answered me when I asked what beverage she wanted.

"I'm a little nervous to be here," she had said when I gave her tea.

"Everyone is a little nervous at first," I had replied. "The Afterlife is not what most people expect."

"The Afterlife?"

Then the tears came. She became a sobbing mess. Her head fell limp on the surface of the table as she cried into the crook of her elbow.

I pushed the tea closer to her. "Have a sip. It'll help." I didn't bother to mention it probably would taste odd. She didn't react, so I kept up the encouragement.

"It's calming tea." It wouldn't have much effect on her, but I hoped it'd help psychologically.

At that, she looked up. She sniffled, still crying, but she grasped the teacup with both hands. The spirit sat straighter in her chair, holding onto the mug, peering at the liquid inside.

Then she turned her attention to me. "Is it poison?"

"No, of course not," I replied calmly.

Her breathing staggered as she sniffled again, taking a sip. Then she placed the cup down as though satisfied with the beverage, but it didn't seem she had drank much at all.

"Take a moment to gather your thoughts and feelings," I said. "You're safe here."

"Safe?" she questioned, rubbing her face with her hands.

I nodded.

"But I thought you said this was the Afterlife?"

"It is."

"But I'm here to die."

I pressed my lips together tightly. Now I saw why she was so upset. She was preparing for death, not realizing it had already happened.

I cleared my throat. "Well, actually, you're here because you're already dead."

"But I don't know what happened to me," she replied, staring at me with pleading eyes. "Did you kill me?"

"No, I did not," I replied.

"How did I get here?"

80

"Well, I helped you find this place."

"And you had nothing to do with my dying?"

"I had nothing to do with you dying," I established.

She turned her gaze out the window, her shoulders hunched over. I didn't know if she believed me or not, but at least the crying had stopped.

"Do you know what happened to me?" she questioned, still looking out at nothing.

"I don't," I responded. That was, of course, a lie.

"I was at work," she stated absentmindedly. "I never thought I'd die at work. Then again, I never thought about how I'd die. I don't even remember what happened. There was an explosion, I think? A fire? I remember being hot, but that's it."

The spirit leaned against her chair, tilting her head back. She sighed heavily, trying to remember what happened to her. She wasn't wrong about most of it. Her office building caught fire after the adjacent building had an explosion. Unfortunately, she got trapped in her office. No one discovered her until it was too late. She wasn't the only one to lose her life that day.

"If only I didn't go to work that day... I'd still be alive," she muttered, more so to herself than to me.

I knew that wasn't true, but I remained quiet. Her internal clock had run out. If she didn't go to work that day, something else would have happened to her, and she'd still be here with me in the Spirit World. It was fate and there was no changing that, even though those in the Living World assumed their choices made a difference. It made them feel better, though, believing they had some sort of control.

The spirit lifted her head, though her demeanor sagged heavily. "There's no going back, is there?"

I shook my head. "Not in a physical form, no. You can wander the Living World as a spirit though."

"And do what?" she released an exhausted snicker. "What's the point? I was going back to school to better my career. I couldn't afford it though and got a second job... the job that killed me. I never figured out my purpose in life. I never figured out why I was born. Now I'm never going to know. My life didn't amount to anything and now it's over. End of story."

She rambled on and I let her. I could share some words of wisdom, but she clearly had a lot to get off her chest.

"I worked and worked and for what? To pay bills? To pay for a house I'll never get to own? I spent so much of my time working, making money, so I could go to school and get a better job so I could make more money. Then, I'd be able to live comfortably and do things I wanted. Have fun. Live life. None of that came to be. Instead, my idea of bettering my life killed me in the end. I amounted to nothing. My life was meaningless."

I frowned, listening to her words. It was rare when I had a soul disappointed with their life rather than upset about what they left behind. This spirit was not only upset that she had died, but upset she couldn't find solace in her life.

Before I could interject with anything, The Clock turned red. It was abrupt, breaking me out of my thoughts. I had never seen that happen so quick, especially when the spirit was so regretful.

As if The Clock spoke to her, she stood and dismissed herself without another word.

I watched her leave, disappointed we didn't chat much. But that was how some sessions went. This spirit was so resigned to her fate to the point she accepted it, keeping her peace far out of reach.

***

Death expectedly happened to everyone. Everyone knew it could strike at any moment. Anyone who was still alive knew not to take life for granted, but that was always easier said than done. Somewhere along the road, those in the Living World had tunnel vision about the things they wanted and went for it. Or they didn't go for it at all.

I wasn't here to judge who did a good job in the Living World and who didn't. Who can say one life was better than another? Every life is unique. Besides, even if I could judge their actions, what good would that do now? These souls meant to find peace in the Afterlife, not mull over what they did or didn't do when they were alive.

Of course, that was the toughest part. Many spirits who arrived here were so concerned about their previous lives—someone they left behind, something they never got to do. The list goes on.

But now it was my job to help turn their thinking around.

The soul sitting at the table with me sipped her tea gingerly. She entered the room as though we'd been good friends for a long time. She was young and, if you asked the Living

World, she was much too young to die. There were no age rules to dying, but the Living World didn't understand that. Regardless, she didn't seem upset in the slightest that she was here.

"What type of tea is this?" she asked, breaking the long silence.

"Chamomile. I don't get too fancy with it since your taste buds are diminishing," I answered.

She smiled. "Well, it tastes delicious anyway."

I held a steady gaze on her. I couldn't read her expression, unsure if she was trying to butter me up for something. Some spirits were like that—they'd act at peace only to fall apart at the end when they realize there's no going back. This was their way of bargaining with me for their life.

"You know, the Afterlife isn't what I thought it'd be," she said, gazing around the room. The teacup remained close to her lips as she gripped tightly to the mug.

"You're not the only one who thinks that," I stated. "What did you think it'd be like?"

She shrugged, still not looking at me. "My parents were religious, so they had this picture perfect vision of heaven. They told me all about it when I was a kid. I believed them, especially since I needed to be on my best behavior or else I'd never get to see heaven." She chuckled. "Now that I'm here, I realize they were wrong. So wrong. I don't know what my mother is going to think when she arrives here."

I smirked. It was a story I've heard time and time again. "Your parents aren't the only ones. Everyone has a different interpretation of what the Afterlife may be like."

"As I grew older, I sort of stopped believing in heaven, but I never told my parents. I didn't want to shatter their belief. But really, I didn't think the Afterlife would be anything. You know, kind of what it actually looks like, but I wouldn't exist anymore," she explained, placing her teacup on the table. She pushed it toward me, indicating she wanted a refill. So, I did.

"You wouldn't believe my shock when I died, and you showed up," she said, fascinatingly watching the tea fill in her cup.

Except she wasn't shocked at all. When I went to her to bring her here, her soul stood over her physical form, watching it sleep. She seemed fascinated more than anything else, much like how she's fascinated by her tea refilling. I'd be lying if I said she didn't look a bit relieved over her dead body.

In some cases, people were afraid of death because they thought they'd no longer exist. Time running out seemed dire. So, when their soul separates from their physical form and they have that out-of-body experience, they realize they're not disappearing. They're not evaporating. Things didn't quite end as they thought it would. In a way, it helps them be a little more accepting of death.

"My life was so hectic," she continued. "When I got sick, and I wasn't able to do anything, I was somewhat relieved. It was a break, in a way. Not a good break, but I had a good excuse for why people couldn't reach out and ask me to do things for them, you know?" she took a sip of tea. "When I found out I didn't have much time left, I was nervous, but I wasn't scared. Does that many sense?"

I nodded. "You wanted the relief at the end, I get that. There is nothing wrong with wanting to rest when you can no longer do anything productive in your physical form."

"You mean my body?"

"You are your soul. The body is simply a host. It's the soul's physical form."

She furrowed her brows, deep in thought. "So, then, the body can't do anything to the soul?"

"No, it's separate. But, obviously, if a physical form can no longer work, the soul needs to leave. It can't do anything in the Living World without a host."

"But how can a broken body kill a soul?"

"The soul isn't killed," I corrected. "It has nowhere else to go, so it comes to the Afterlife. People in the Living World believe the body and soul are the same, but they're very different from one another. The body cannot live without the soul, but the soul continues living without the body. It can't remain doing all the same things it did because because the soul has no sense of taste, touch, or smell. A soul can't go to work, drive a car, or do anything. Since it can't do the basic things to remain in the Living World and those still alive can't see souls, they presume the spirit to be dead. Thus, there's no place for spirits in the Living World."

The soul paused for a moment, taking in my words. She sipped her tea casually and then let out another snicker. "Wow, we really got the whole life and death thing wrong, huh?"

"To many, seeing is believing. Others believe in something through faith and their feelings. Believing in something is good. It doesn't matter if your belief is correct. If you believe in something, it gives you cause to keep pressing forward. It encourages you to always do the right thing, even though your version of the right thing may be wrong to someone else."

"We live our lives based on belief and argue with those who don't agree with our opinions," she added bluntly, though a glint of amusement filled her eyes. "Someone always has to be right and then things get complicated when there's a differing of opinion."

That was an understatement. I couldn't describe how complicated the Living World made living.

"So, being dead is like being alive, but without the stress?" she questioned, curiosity piquing her tone.

"Yes," I answered. The only stress that existed in the Spirit World was for those who didn't quite accepted their death yet and hadn't found their peace. Otherwise, stress wasn't a common feeling in the Afterlife because there were no man-made objects, such as time or currency. Spirits didn't need to worry about their health or harsh weather conditions. The Afterlife was meant for souls to find peace and continue living based on what they wanted to remember from their previous lives. It was a hard concept to grasp for most spirits, though.

"Is there a Beforelife?" she asked, breaking me out of my thoughts.

I stared at her quizzically as she leaned back in her chair, making herself comfortable with her teacup in hand.

"You know," she clarified, waving one hand along, "like the Afterlife, but before we're born into our physical form. If there is, I don't remember it."

I grinned at her out-of-box thinking. "Our spirits can only remember so much. Once one life ends, another soon begins."

She scrunched her face in confusion, staring intensely at me. "So there is a Beforelife?"

"I'm not at liberty to say."

She nodded, though I could tell she wasn't satisfied with my answer. The spirit sipped her tea some more, gazing out the window. After a moment of silence, she turned her attention back to me.

"What's the purpose of all this?"

"The Living World or the Spirit World?" I wondered aloud.

"All of it."

"That's something you must determine on your own."

She hummed to herself, peering into her teacup again. "I died before I reached my forties. I'm not entirely sure what the purpose of my life was. Did I accomplish what I was supposed to do, and that's why I died? Or did I get sick to help someone else and my death was my purpose?"

"Do explain," I prompted.

"My illness was a rare form of some disease. Because of my death, they're able to use my body and organs to run tests and possibly figure out a cure."

I nodded along, listening intently. It interested me to hear a spirit believe their purpose in life was to die. I didn't know what her purpose was because I wasn't aware of the things she did when she was alive. However, she spoke so sincerely about it; I had a feeling she was on the right track. At this time, The Clock turned orange, though she didn't seem to notice.

"If my purpose in life was to die and now I'm still living, that means I need to find a new purpose, right?" She continued speaking into her teacup. "Otherwise, why would we continue living as spirits? Maybe I can go back to the Living World and help the scientists somehow."

I smiled, pleased to know she made a plan for herself. Most spirits weren't ready to jump back into the Living World so soon. This spirit wasn't thinking about her friends and family, though. She thought about the many lives she could extend from having that disease. For someone who found relief in death from helping others, that's still all she thought about.

The Clock turned red at the end of her words and we said our goodbyes.

"I appreciate you taking the time to listen to me," she said before her departure.

"I'm always here if you need anything," I replied.

With little else, she thanked me again and exited the room. I sat back down at the table, staring at the blue rose centerpiece. I couldn't help but smile to myself, knowing a spirit understood that finding their purpose didn't end in death. She'd find her purpose and complete it. Then, she'd unknowingly go back to the Living World with a new purpose.

The truth was, the Beforelife, as she called it, and the Afterlife were the same.

***

"Why give us drinks if we can't taste them anymore?"

"It's more for comfort," I answered. The group session had barely begun, and I got bombarded with questions. "Your senses may still linger."

"So, I could taste this if I wanted to?" the young man asked, closely leaning in to inspect his mug.

I nodded. "It's why you can physically pick up the cup, too."

The three picked up their mugs and drank in silence. Each of them suddenly eager to sip their beverages, hoping for that hint of flavor.

"Would anyone like to share anything?" I asked.

One of the woman raised her hand. "I ended up going back to school."

I grinned. "I'm happy to hear that."

When I last saw this spirit, she did most of the talking if she wasn't crying. I barely got a word in. She was so distraught she didn't get to do what she planned on in life. She had wanted to go back to school and never got the chance. Now that she knew she could go back and forth between here and the Living World, it seemed like she joined a few classes as a spirit.

"There's a school here?" the man questioned, turning his attention to me. I shook my head, but the woman replied.

"I sit in on classes in the Living World," she explained.

"But you won't get a degree," he answered, still baffled.

"No," she said, frowning. "I wouldn't be able to use a degree here, anyway. But I enjoy the knowledge."

She was such a different spirit than before. She sobbed helplessly into the table during our first meeting and now she was living well in the Afterlife.

The man leaned back in his seat, whistling. "I never thought to do that." He pointed at me. "You told me to make amends in death."

"Yes, for you to look at your time in the Living World and use that knowledge to decide what to do here. Ultimately, it's up to you," I stated.

"I went back to the Living World, too," the other woman piped up.

"Am I the only one who hasn't been back there...?" the man groaned.

"I went back to check in on the doctors and scientists with my body. I had a rare disease they're trying to cure," she explained, looking at the other two spirits sitting at the table. "I think my purpose is to help cure that disease."

"Wait," the man held up a hand, looking at me once more. "I asked you what my purpose was, and you said I needed to figure it out myself."

"I didn't say they told me my purpose," the lady replied, jutting a thumb to me but looking at the spirit beside her. "I figured it out through our conversation. Even then, I'm still not sure if it's the right thing."

"But it feels right to you, so you're going with it?" the other woman added.

"Exactly."

The man slouched in his chair, pinching the bridge of his nose. "Let me get this straight... I had a purpose in life, didn't know what it was, and now I'm dead. But I have to find my purpose in death, too? What's the time frame on that?"

"You have all the time to figure it out," the woman replied. "We're dead. I assume there's no more internal clock?" she ended with a question, facing me.

I folded my hands on the table. "May I interject?"

"Yes," the three spirits replied in unison.

"You lived your lives. What you did or didn't do doesn't matter anymore. However, you still have those memories. You remember how they made you feel? When I explained you should take what you learned in the Living World and make amends in the Spirit World, I meant to keep doing what you're doing. Whatever you feel is right. Listen to your gut, even though you no longer have one."

"What sort of choices do we have to make here, though?" the man inquired.

"I can't answer that for you," I replied, shrugging. "Some spirits go back to the Living World to be with their loved ones. Others," I nodded to the spirit sitting beside him, "go back to the Living World to continue the life they wanted." I looked at the other lady. "And others go back to help those still living." I turned my attention to the gentleman. "Finally, some remain in the Spirit World, taking their time going back, or never going back at all. There's no right or wrong answer, only what you feel is best for you."

The man sighed. "But I don't know what feels best. I'm not sure I feel anything anymore. My whole life has been a lie, and it ended prematurely. I had no purpose in life and now I don't know what to do."

"You must have had a purpose or else you wouldn't have been born," one woman said.

The other lady added her piece. "The point is, you're here now and you need to make the most of it."

I watched the trio converse as one would watch a tennis match. This group session didn't go as I thought it would, but the conversation didn't go sour. The two ladies knew what they wanted. To them, if they were wrong, they'd be able to fix it here. Since they were dead, they believed they had all the time in the world.

The gentleman felt uneasy. Confusion clouded his judgment. The ladies were determined to go with the flow to find their peace, while the man wanted to get it right the first time.

Yet, The Clock turned orange.

The man stood from his seat, smiling at the women. "You know, I think I need to take pages out of your books. I don't know why I died when I did. I don't know if I accomplished my life's purpose. If I did, it was an accident. But I'm here now and need to move forward."

"Yes!" one woman cheered.

"So, what are you going to do now?" the other asked.

It was as though I was no longer in the room.

"I don't know," he replied honestly. "Maybe explore this place a little more before exploring what the Living World now offers me."

The Clock turned red, and they all stood to leave. They conversed with one another, thanking me for my time before leaving. I didn't feel I did too much, though. Some of these group sessions felt I wasn't needed. The spirits worked together to get themselves through this moment. This isn't a complaint—I was proud of them.

But I couldn't help but wonder... did I have a purpose?

THE SEVENTH GROUP

"88 YEARS. I NEVER imagined my life would have lasted that long. There was so much left to do, yet there was nothing at all. I had three children, eight grandchildren, and two great-grandchildren. I guess there was a lot left for me.

"But my body couldn't function anymore. My knees ached day and night. I could barely walk. My cane helped a little, but I couldn't drive anymore. I couldn't garden. Even my eyes grew bad that I couldn't read as much as I wanted.

"I watched TV a lot. Loud. I think it bothered the others in the house. Even with my hearing aids in, it was difficult for me to hear the television. But I'll admit, I sometimes turned my hearing aids off to drown out the other sounds in the house."

He chuckled.

"I liked watches. They used the same batteries as my hearing aids, so I'd take the batteries from my aids and use them to replace the dead batteries from my watches. But even that got difficult to do overtime. My hands shook, and those batteries were so damn small.

"As you can see, it's weird to imagine I had lasted 88 years. But, I guess, despite my body failing me, I was determined to stay with my family. I got to watch my children make wonderful families. I got to spoil my grandchildren and great-grandchildren. I watched most of them grow up.

"But the longer you live, the more you witness. Watching my family grow was a beautiful experience. I grew old with my wife, even though she stopped remembering me in the end. She got dementia, you know. But I'm grateful for the good times and for all the memories I got to keep with me.

"Boy, did we make a lot of memories. My family took summer vacations by a lake every year. We brought the dogs, of course. These vacations were wonderful. We had lots of fun. Lots of laughs."

He held up his glass as a toast. When I had asked what beverage he wanted, he specifically requested scotch on the rocks. I obliged, knowing the alcohol wouldn't affect him as a spirit. This gentleman was already at peace and simply wanted to share his story.

I clinked my glass with his, and he downed his drink. Only then did The Clock turn red.

***

"Are you sure you meant to take me? What about my brother? He's older than me. How did I go before him?"

I stared at the ripples in my coffee cup as I placed the mug down on the table. This lady couldn't understand that I didn't *take* her from anywhere. I had explained to her everyone has a certain amount of time to live from the moment they're born into the Living World. I didn't know how long each person had and I had no control over it. Yet, she didn't believe me. I decided it was best to let her talk. Get her thoughts out and arrive at her own conclusions about her eternal situation.

"I was always careful. A good person. My brother is a good person, too, but he was a wild teenager. If anyone should have their life cut short, it should have been him... no offense."

Believe it or not, this wasn't the first encounter I had with a soul where they wished one of their loved ones took their place. I knew the spirit before me didn't actually mean it. I didn't think she understood what her words meant. She panicked, so she rambled. Her shock about her demise spiraled.

"I mean, I guess I don't wish for my brother to be dead," she said.

"Of course not," I replied calmly.

"I just don't get it. I thought if someone was older than you, they'd naturally go first. I've prepared for that." She leaned forward on the table, tracing the rim of her teacup with an index finger.

"Prepared for what, exactly?" I inquired.

"His death."

I raised a brow. This was certainly a first. I don't think I've ever met a soul who thought so much about death as long as it wasn't their own.

"He's in his fifties now. It's only a matter of time," she shrugged.

"I wouldn't consider that old."

"It's not old at all."

"But it's an age where death is around the corner?"

She paused, glancing upward. Then she sat straight, sipping her tea. "No, I suppose not. He just wasn't getting any younger. None of us were."

"How many of you were there?"

"Four. My brother, myself, and twin sisters younger than me. Both my parents are alive, too. I certainly didn't expect them to outlive me."

Her confusion made more sense. It was tough when a spirit arrived in the Afterlife before their parents. It wasn't that the person wished their parents to go, but it wasn't part of the circle of life, as the Living World affectionately called it. Naturally, parents went before their children because they were much older. However, the universe often had other plans. When in the Living World, one must play the game of life as best they can. It's a difficult thing to do when you don't know the rules, but that's also part of the game.

"So," she continued, interrupting my thoughts, "as you can see, there must have been some mistake."

"Unfortunately, no," I replied calmly. "You're here because your time was up."

"Can't you give me a little more time?"

I shook my head. She had already been here for so long anyway that even if I held that power, she'd go back as someone else.

She threw her head back, releasing a long, loud groan.

Denial was never a fun part of grief. Some spirits snapped out of it faster than others, but there were some that took much longer. I didn't blame them, of course. It is a difficult concept to grasp. Despite what they believed in the Living World, the Spirit World was much different. No matter what they say or do, no matter how much they beg or manifest, there's no changing their situation. All they can do is make the best of it.

"Can I speak to the person in charge?" she asked, lifting her head to stare at me.

"Excuse me?" That was a new one.

"You said you don't have any control over who dies and stuff, so can I speak to who is?"

I paused, trying to understand what she wanted. "You mean the universe?"

Her eyes widened. "I can speak to the universe?"

"No."

"Then why'd you suggest it?"

"I wasn't," I sighed. "Let me put it this way; when something went wrong in your life and you wanted to change it, what did you do?"

"I figured it out."

I nodded.

"Or I asked my parents or siblings for help, but they're not here. But also, if something went wrong in the grocery store, for example, I'd ask to speak to a manager. So, where's your manager?"

"There is no manager in death."

"Everyone has a manager."

"That's not how it works here."

"Then you're the manager? Of this place?"

Honestly, I never thought about it before. I was the only one around, aside from all the other spirits. As the Grim Reaper, it was my job to guide everyone to cross over peacefully. I never thought that made me the manager of the Afterlife.

"I guess so?" I didn't like the sound of it, but maybe it's what she needed to hear.

"There's no one above you I could speak to?" she asked.

I shook my head.

She slouched in her chair, twisting her head away.

We sat in silence for who knows how long. I sipped my coffee while she pouted. Normally, I'd say something, but her denial ran so deep I didn't think there was anything I could do to help. We were at the point in the conversation where she needed to turn the discussion and talk herself through her thoughts.

"Am I stuck here?"

She finally broke the silence and, when I looked at her, she remained staring out into the void through the window.

"Yes." It was the most honest answer I could give.

Her head bowed, somber. "How did this happen to me?" she whispered. "I don't understand how life ended up this way."

It didn't end up in any way. It ended.

"There's nothing left for me to do then, huh? I'm here and that's that." It wasn't a question. She had become dejected of her fate.

"You have free will here," I explained gently. "Stay and rest here for a while, which I'm sure your mind and spirit deserve. You can mingle with other souls; find lost loved ones and meet new friends. Or you can explore the Living World as a spirit. Be with your siblings and parents. When it's time for them to join us here, you can help guide them."

She pursed her lips together, her gaze scanning the room. "Can I visit them now?" she asked, finally landing her eyes on me.

I nodded.

"What about my funeral?"

"You can attend that if you'd like."

She chuckled. "I wonder who will show up."

It interested me how that was often a first thought for many souls. It made sense to be curious about who would arrive at the funeral to say a last goodbye, but it was also the human nature still inside them from when they were alive. Even in death, they were still thinking about themselves.

"Will they know I'm there?" she asked.

"If they pay attention, they will," I replied.

"What if they don't pay attention?"

"Not everyone will," I said with a shrug. "It all depends on what they believe in. Even if they believe in the Spirit World, they may not always have their eyes or their mind open to it. I think they lose it overtime the longer a loved one is gone, which is why I believe it's important to visit them often. With that said, from what I've experienced with other spirits, I've noticed that their loved ones—whether they believe in spirits or not—are way more receptive to watching out for signs soon after their loved one moves on."

She nodded along with my words, sipping her tea. "So, you're saying if I'm going to visit at all, I should do it now?"

"They'll be more likely to see the signs, yes."

"And if I want them to know I'm always around, I should visit often?"

"That's what seems to work the best."

"What if they don't listen?"

"No one can listen all the time. That'll depend on them and what's going on in their lives."

"What does that mean?" she asked, sitting forward.

I shifted my weight in my seat. "Well, it varies from person to person. If someone is stressed, they might be more inclined to look for help from the Spirit World. They might outright ask for a sign to let them know things will eventually turn out alright. Another person could be so stressed that they have tunnel vision. Whether they ask for the help, they're blinded by the stress and miss the signs all together. They're too worried, too wrapped up in whatever they're dealing with."

The woman put a hand to her cheek, thinking. "I think I get it." She stood. "I'll visit my family soon. I'm sure they're going to need all the help they can get grieving their loss of me."

And there she was, thinking about herself again. However, she probably wasn't wrong. She had died in her forties from a strange illness. It was unexpected, so her family probably suffered confusion as they mourned.

I only hoped she decided to help her family for them rather than for her own sake and peace of mind.

***

"It's weird, isn't it?"

"What is?"

"One moment they're here and the next... they're gone."

"I know. We had a lovely conversation last night. So, when I got the phone call this morning saying they'd..."

"But they're not in pain anymore. It was quick. I'm almost... happy for them, you know?"

"Quick? They've been in the hospital for two months."

"Right, but the actual death was quick. And no one wants to spend the rest of their life in a hospital."

"Can you see me?"

The third voice jolted me out of my eavesdropping. It wasn't like me to linger and listen in on the living, but I watched the newly departed spirit watch over their family. I looked at them as they looked me up and down.

I nodded.

"Are you here to take me home?" they asked.

"That's depends; which home do you mean?"

"Not this one." They looked over their shoulder at their family members still conversing, unaware of our presence. "My family can't hear me anymore."

I guided the spirit to the Afterlife, and they joined me in the Crossover Room right away. They gazed out into the abyss through the mock window beside the table.

"So, this is it?" they muttered to themselves.

I peered into my coffee mug, watching the steam delicately rise into the air. Normally, I read a spirit's emotions well, but this one? I was unsure.

"This is what death is like? What a joke."

They were numb. I didn't know if it was from grief or secret relief.

"Quick? Painless? Is that something the living tells themselves to make them feel better about someone else dying?"

Yes. Yes, it was. But I didn't dare say that out loud.

"I guess I shouldn't be angry. I said that many times to people who had lost loved ones. They're in a better place... they're resting... they're happy..." they described in a mocking tone. "But now I know the truth. It's not quick. The journey here sucked."

I turned my gaze away from my mug and stared at the spirit's profile. I couldn't read their full expression, but judging from their harsh tone, it was obvious they felt a mixture of anger and sadness.

"Until you came along, I mean," they added casually. "It took me a minute to realize you were there for me. Before I left my body, though, that... well, that part wasn't quick is all."

I nodded, despite them not looking at me. They were right. The soul leaving its physical form was a rough process. It wasn't as quick as blinking or as painless as falling asleep. The soul and body were connected in ways no one could ever understand.

The soul doesn't rise from the body discreetly and carefully, as the Living World depicts in movies. It rips itself free. The physical form doesn't want to let go. It holds on tight, the heart and brain always the last to loosen its grip.

But the soul doesn't want to leave, either. It doesn't fly out of its physical form because it's ready to move on. The Spirit World pulls it through to the other side. When time is up, when the internal clock turns red, that's it. There's no going back, no changing fate's mind.

The body and soul are woven together into a beautiful tapestry of individuality. Every death on the outside is different, but on the inside? It's a struggle. The soul doesn't want to leave, but it has no choice. The body doesn't understand what's happening until it's too late.

"It wasn't painless, either," they continued, unaware I was lost in my own thoughts. "All those months spend in the hospital... even on my good days, I lay in bed struggling to move. I couldn't breathe. I suffocated."

I didn't understand the extent of this spirit's illness when they were alive. All I know was that by the time they were diagnosed, it was too late. The disease was terminal. They had a few months left to live. Unfortunately, after three weeks, the illness took a turn, and they spent their last months in a hospital room.

"I think I get it, though," they stated, turning away from the abyss to peer into their mug. "No one wants to see their loved ones suffering. But it makes me wonder... were they happy I was at peace or because it finally brought them peace?"

I leaned forward, folding my arms on the table. "Do you think they don't grieve for you?"

They glared at me. "That's not what I mean. When you're sick in the hospital, bedridden, it takes a toll on those who care for you. You become a burden. They tell you you're not, but it's all lies for your benefit. The hospital is the last place they want to be. Seeing you in a hospital, vulnerable, hooked up to beeping machines... it's the last place they want to keep you company.

"Now that I'm gone, they don't need to worry about that anymore. No more hospitals. No more figuring out who's going to visit me and when. No more meetings with doctors or wondering what pill they should give me next." They looked at me, their gaze no longer filled with rage, but overflowing with sadness now.

However, a small smile formed across their lips. "When the living says the dead are at peace, they're not talking about the dead. They think they are, but they're not. We're confused. We're alone. We're grieving for what we've lost. But the living... they smile through the pain and tell themselves we're better off. That's how they get through the sadness. Because if they tell themselves the deceased is okay... well, they'll believe just about anything if it makes them feel better."

It was rare a spirit was so completely aware of the bridge between the living and the dead. It was true; the Living World told themselves many stories about the dead they believed to be true. If they didn't have anything to believe in, then what was the point of moving on? They needed that hope to give them strength to move forward.

"What a selfish thing to do," they muttered scornfully.

My eyes widened in surprise. "Selfish?"

They nodded, following up with another smirk. "I'm not completely innocent, though. I lied, you know."

I remained silent, intrigued by what they'd say next.

"I said my family couldn't hear me anymore, but who's to say if they could or couldn't?"

I knew the answer to that. They wouldn't be able to, no matter how loud they screamed. I didn't dare respond, though.

They looked at me, forcing a smile. "I never called out to them. I couldn't. When they got the call I was gone, not a single tear had been shed. They were happy for me, thinking this is what I wanted. Thinking I was better off, no longer in pain, at peace or whatever. They were all finally free. Free from the burden that was me and my illness.

"And it was at that moment I realized I was free, too. Honestly, I haven't felt this good in a long time. Not since before the illness took over. Although I'm not happy with the outcome. There were many things I still wanted to do. I still hurt, yearning to speak to my loved ones again. But I'm free and so are they, so... I guess peace will come soon enough."

The Clock turned red, and they stood as though they knew it was time to go. They exited the room without another word, without so much as a glance in my direction. Whatever they'd do next was a mystery to me.

Their loved ones shed tears, but they did so in private. While they didn't want to be a burden to their loved ones, the family didn't want to show fear or pity.

The living told themselves the deceased went quickly and painlessly because it made them feel better. It often confused the spirit, sometimes angered them. What they didn't realize was that they did the same thing. Telling themselves they were no longer a burden to their loved ones was the same as the living telling themselves the dead was no longer in pain.

***

"What did you die from?" the elderly gentleman asked.

"I was sick."

"An illness."

He nodded as the two other spirits replied in unison.

"This gentleman was in hospice when I arrived to bring him to the Afterlife," I explained, attempting to move the conversation along.

"Oh," one woman replied, turning her attention to the man. "You were sick, too?"

"No," he chuckled, "just old."

The other soul scoffed, folding her arms defensively. "You're lucky. You got to live your full life. I got sick and spent my last few months in a hospital bed with my family and friends, wasting their time by my bedside."

The man frowned. "It doesn't sound like they wasted their time at all. My family did the same for me when I was in the hospital and then again when I moved to hospice. They talked to me. Reminded me how much they loved me. I don't know if they know, but I heard every word. They grieved for me before I left, but it helped me find my peace before I made it here. I'm sure your family did the same."

The soul dropped their hands to their lap, their expression changing. I got the feeling they didn't want to admit that there was an inkling the gentleman may be right.

"And just because I'm old doesn't mean I lived a full life. I had a wonderful life, of course. I'm proud of it. I'm proud of my family. But I had to give up many things because of my old age. I couldn't do the things I loved anymore," he continued explaining.

The other spirits in the room leaned closer, listening intently.

"Walking grew to be a struggle. I couldn't read my books anymore as my eyes worsened. All I could do was sit and watch TV."

The other soul leaned back in their chair, sighing. "I couldn't do anything either after a while. Once my sickness got hold of me, that was it."

He smiled. "But you still had your family by your side, didn't you?"

"Yeah, but—"

"Did you love them?"

"Of course I did."

"And they loved you?"

"Well, I should hope so if they decided spending their free time at the hospital."

He grinned at the response. "It's not ideal. No one wants to spend their time watching a loved one suffer. My last night at home I asked my son to give me one final night in my bed. I knew I wouldn't be coming back. I spent my last month at the hospital and then at the hospice house. It was a long, grueling month for me and my family. But I don't think my family would have had it any other way. We worked together to overcome those feelings and situations. I'm sure your family wouldn't have changed anything, either. They did what they wanted to do, and that was being there for you."

The other soul cracked a small smile, nodding their head. They pressed their lips together, hiding their expression behind their drink.

Finally, the woman reached out to the gentleman. "Did you have any siblings?"

"I did," he answered.

"Younger than you? Did any of them die first?"

He nodded. "I was the youngest and all my siblings went before me, sadly. But I had a younger brother. He got sick as a baby and passed away."

"A... baby?"

"Yes."

"Oh..." she muttered, deflating in her chair. "I guess my age doesn't seem nearly as bad now."

"It's a shock," I chimed in on the conversation. "There's no telling how long someone will remain in the Living World. No one knows how long they have until their time is up."

"Why does it work like that?" she asked.

"I'm not sure. I don't make the rules. You need to learn how to live your life while you're living it. It's tough not knowing the end goal until after you've finished playing the game, but I imagine you all reached some sort of goal in your lifetime."

"I watched my family grow and had a successful career," the old man replied. "I wouldn't have changed my life for anything."

The other spirit nodded along. "I didn't have a family of my own, but I traveled a lot with my family members and friends. The ending was sour, but I guess I wouldn't change anything leading up to it."

"And I'm grateful for the time my family will get that I didn't. It's weird being here and not there with them, but I guess you're right. I wouldn't change anything leading up to this moment."

The Clock turned red. I found it to be too soon, but it seemed the gentleman's words stuck with the other spirits. He wasn't wrong. Everyone in the Living World needed to work together to get themselves through situations, no matter what it was.

The Spirit World was no different. We all needed to be there for one another, too.

ACKNOWLEDGEMENTS

Apparitions Anonymous came to be because of a random thought I had. I shared a few stories on my website and realized I enjoyed writing about such themes. I had more ideas and kept writing them. Thus, this book was born. These stories come from the heart and I hope you read them with an open mind and learned something from them or even view life a little differently now. It feels like everyone is always in a rush these days and I hope these stories serve as a friendly reminder to slow down, enjoy every moment, and spend time with your loved ones because we don't know what tomorrow brings.

Of course, this book didn't come to life only because of my idea. I had the encouragement and support from my family and friends. Not only did they support me through the writing and making of the book, but they also had to endure my rambling and stress about it, too.

I also want to thank my online fellow writers who supported me through my many Instagram posts about the book—you know who you are! But I have to give a special shout out to Ari. Not only has she been with me on my writing journey for years, but she's heard me talk about this book from the very beginning. Plus, she spread the word about this book and encouraged me to talk about it and, you know, do author-like things for it when I didn't think to (or was too nervous to).

My Caffeinated Club on Ko-fi also made this book possible, so a huge thank you to Kris and Mom.

I can't forget to thank you, my readers, for making it through this book. Thank you for being interested enough in the book to get a copy, let alone read through it. If you get a chance, please leave a review where you bought the book; it'll help me grow as an author and I'd love to hear your thoughts on these stories.

Finally, I need to give a shout out to myself. (Don't roll your eyes. I'm not being arrogant; I promise.) The fact I sat down, wrote a book, and actually published it—sticking to my deadlines, mind you—is a big deal in itself. My excitement for this book never faltered, and these stories came from the heart. Apparitions Anonymous was cathartic for me and I didn't know I had it in me to write such pieces. I'm proud of what I've accomplished and I hope these stories touched your heart and made a lasting positive impact. Thank you again so much for reading.

ABOUT THE AUTHOR

Rachel Poli is a cozy mystery and paranormal author, writing short stories, novels, and the occasional flash fiction piece.

Her work explores the obscurities of life through themes of love, loss, and mental health. These stories unleash genuine emotion that will leave you with deep thoughts.

In her spare time, she's usually organizing something or playing video games with a coffee in hand. She lives in New England with her zoo.

***

Connect with Rachel

Website: RachelPoliAuthor.com
Join the Caffeinated Club: Ko-fi.com/RachelPoli
Instagram: @RachelP_Reads

BOOKS BY RACHEL POLI

The Grim Reaper Files

Apparitions Anonymous
Happily Ever Afterlife (releasing 2025)

Flash Fiction

Sunday Morning

Catch a sneak peek of more crossover sessions from book two in The Grim Reaper Files

Releasing October 2025

HAPPILY EVERY AFTERLIFE

The Grim Reaper Files, book 2

A blue rose sat in a tall, thin vase on the table's surface. It never needed watering. Never wilted. It barely had a scent.

I remember when I added the blue flower as a centerpiece. One soul I had encountered in this room talked about decorating the place. She thought the Crossover Room was her bedroom, even though it wasn't. No one has their own space here. We all mingle together as one, coming and going between the Spirit World and the Living World as we please.

However, her thoughts in decorating got me thinking. I spend most of my time in this room. Why shouldn't it have a little ambiance? Why shouldn't it be a little more homey? Comforting? For me and for the many spirits that come here.

Yet, the rose was an odd reminder that I was always here. Ironically, spirits come into this room to meet with me about where to find their place in the Afterlife. Or where to find their place in the Living World while in their spirit form.

Where was my place? Was it here? Was it always going to be here? I couldn't remember how I got to this point. The flower was stuck here just as much as I was.

Would I change anything? No, not at all. I enjoyed my work; meeting the many spirits, even though some sessions were difficult. I didn't mind helping these souls overcome their fear, confusion, and grief. Many of these spirits had taken their living lives for granted, and I didn't want them to take this new form for granted, either.

So, when my next soul entered the room, glaring at my blue rose, I didn't know what to think. They had refused a beverage—even hot chocolate. I didn't give myself a drink so as not to be rude. We sat in silence for a long time; them glaring at my flower, unblinking. I had tried starting a conversation many times, but nothing came of it.

I had the occasional session where the soul barely spoke a work to me. Once, I had a soul speak entirely to themselves. They thought I was a hallucination. The session had gone well enough because they talked themselves through their issues and found a solution for themselves. It was weirdly the easiest and most difficult session I ever had.

This soul didn't speak at all, though. They barely looked at me, only focused on the flower.

"Do you like it?" I asked.

No response. Not even a flinch.

I leaned back in my chair, getting comfortable. The Clock remained green, and I knew it would stay that way for some time. There was little sense in me staying on guard when it was clear the spirit needed to come to me in their own time.

After a few moments, they laid their arms down on the table, resting their chin on the crook of their elbow. Their eyes locked with the vase, brows furrowed.

What were they thinking? They no longer looked angry at the flower, but were highly interested in it. If I had known the flower would have had such an impact, I might not have had it at all. Unless, of course, it was a positive impact.

The spirit looked like a child, resting their head on the windowsill as if waiting up for Santa Claus. With that thought, I had an idea. I waved my hand slightly and changed the color of the rose to pink.

The soul's eyes widened, impressed. I detected a small smile on their face, too. So, I changed the color to yellow. The soul grinned. Green, red, orange, and then finally, rainbow. The spirit sat up, giggling.

"Do you like it?" I asked again.

They nodded. "I've never seen anything like it. What flower shop did you get it from?"

I shook my head. "No flower shop here. I made it myself."

"You grew it in your garden?"

"Sure."

"You've got one hell of a green thumb." They rested their chin on the table again, staring in awe at the colorful petals.

"Did you like flowers in the Living World?" I questioned, urging the conversation to continue.

The spirit nodded as best as they could with their head on the table. "I had a garden in my backyard. It was massive. Had a greenhouse and everything. I grew lots of things.

Veggies, fruits, flowers... if you can stick it in the ground and grow something new from it, you bet that's what I did. Bringing something to life is an amazing feeling."

"I bet it is."

"Well, you should know," they said, lifting their head to look at me. "You grew this flower."

"I did." I didn't. Not in the way they assumed, anyway. But I'd let this spirit think what they needed to.

"Gardening made me so happy. Plants are living creatures, you know."

"They are," I agreed.

"They breathe like we do. They drink water, soak up vitamin D... most plants are smart enough to grow toward the sun. Did you know that?"

"That's amazing," I replied, pretending I didn't already know that.

The spirit sat up again, leaning back in their chair. "Plants don't have the same worries and stresses as humans do."

Unless they had a person who forgot to water them, but I nodded along anyway.

"They're only focus is to grow. Better themselves."

Huh. I wasn't expecting this perspective, but I liked where the conversation headed.

"I think all humans can learn from plants. Some are prickly, some aren't. Others have beautiful colors, while some are quite dull. But they all have personality and keep growing tall. It's amazing!"

"Absolutely. I've never thought about plants in that way before."

"Some smell amazing and other don't. You can eat some of them, too. Although, I don't know if they'd appreciate that much..."

I chuckled at their rambling. They brought up decent points, but I was just happy they were talking.

"I wanted to keep growing. Better myself, just like the plants in my garden," they continued.

"Did you?" I questioned.

They frowned. "I don't know. If you ask my friends and family, they'd tell you no. I think I did, though. It was hard for me to get out of my comfort zone, but I tried whenever someone wanted to do something. I couldn't keep friendships or relationships well because of that. It was difficult for me. The only thing I felt I could do right was take care of my plants.

"I kept myself well fed and watered. I had good hygiene habits. I spent a lot of time outside in the sun—tending to my garden, you know. But, for some reason, many people didn't think that was right for me. They wanted me to go out. They wanted me to meet new people, try new things. But then they'd complain when I met someone and talked about my plants. I don't know why they cared so much. I did what I wanted and what I liked. It made me happy when others wanted to share that with me, but they'd get sick of it overtime."

I nodded along as they spoke. It was all too common when spirits came to me discussing how others wanted them to change in the Living World. Most of the time, humans didn't grow and improve because they wanted to, but because others wanted them to. The Living World was obsessed with appearances and behaving a certain way, especially in front of certain groups. It upset me to listen to these stories because most of the times; the spirit didn't do what they wanted or what made them happy. They recounted their tale on the whim of other people without taking their own feelings into account.

It was all too easy for those in the Living World to lose themselves. They're all born innocent and unique, but equal to others. Yet, as they grow older, as they meet new people and encounter certain situations, they worry about what others think. They do what others want them to do. Unfortunately, almost all humans went through those motions—they had to lose themselves first before discovering who they are.

"Would you change anything about your life?" I wondered aloud. To me, it sounded as though this spirit took their interests in stride. They shared it with others and, when no one wanted to reciprocate, this soul moved on, staying true to themselves.

"Not at all," they replied confidently, with a smile.

"You were happy?"

"Of course."

"Then I wouldn't worry too much about what others think, about why they didn't appreciate your plants as much as you did."

They waved their hand dismissively with a laugh. "Oh, I don't worry about that. Plants have no worries, so why should I? It's the only way to live life well. Take things day by day. I was still nice to those people, even if they thought I was weird. Be kind to your neighbors, you know? Companion planting is important. It makes a world of difference."

I couldn't help but laugh. No matter what was on this spirit's mind, plants always sneaked back into the conversation. I had to give them credit, though. Plants could teach us a lot about living. More than I realized.

"I'm glad you have flowers here," they continued, watching the rose again. "No offense, but it's kind of dreary here. Having flowers might help some souls feel better. More comfortable."

"That's what I'm going for," I agreed, even though the flower was someone else's idea.

The Clock turned red. I hadn't realized the session neared its end, but it was clear to me now that this spirit was fine with their situation. Maybe knowing flowers exist in the Afterlife was all the comfort they needed. We said our goodbyes to each other and, as I watched them leave, I couldn't help but wonder if someone in the Living World still took care of their garden.